FULL BODY MANSLAUGHTER

A FARRAH WETHERS MYSTERY

ELIZABETH AMBER LOVE

Printed Edition ISBN: 0998061506
Printed Edition ISBN-13: 978-0-9980615-0-4

To my beloved and missed Caico.

CHAPTER ONE

SUNDAY

FARRAH grabbed the four sets of scrubs she owned and placed them in the suitcase. When she turned her back to sort through the underwear and socks she needed, Miles the ginger cat, saw his chance to try and pack himself.

"Oh, my sweet old boy, you can't go with me. I wish you could."

She gave him some scratches behind his ears and packed the socks around him making a nest. The rest of the bed had organized piles of plastic zipper bags filled with soap, shampoo, and toothpaste. Farrah laid out a few outfits having no idea what to wear to a corporate retreat.

"I think I need more coffee, Miles. I need something to stimulate my brain cells to make a decision." The cat had nestled successfully and didn't seem to care what she needed at that moment.

"Fine. Stay there." He was as loyal as most house cats. His priority was that he had Farrah's attention more than Gordon the bloodhound who invaded their domicile not too long ago.

She took a long look at the piles and saw chaos. Decisions waited to be made. To anyone else, it would have looked like a neatly organized plan in action.

Coffee cravings beckoned. She pulled her shoulders back from the hunch they had fallen into before leaving the bedroom.

There wasn't much to the Sunday morning sunrise. It was grey and dismal, just another November day in New Jersey. The window shades were cracked open allowing enough light to filter in so she wouldn't trip along her route through the hallway and down the stairs.

In the living room, she found Jackson still asleep on the couch and Gordon on the big dog pillow next to him. Farrah tried to keep her footsteps light, but the old floors had a way of creaking worse the more careful she tried to be.

When she reached the dining room's coffee bar, her hand grabbed the carafe. As soon as she ran the water, the dog was alerted to the presence of an awake human who could feed him and lumbered after her slowly, showing signs of his age.

The massive dog stood next to Farrah in a way that would have been creepy if he were another person. The dog had serious personal boundary issues. She knew deep inside that he was only trying to be affectionate and wanted some love in return, but since Jackson brought him home without so much as asking her thoughts on the matter, she harbored resentment.

She huffed once knowing she was being an ass and had to rise above ill will over a dog. She turned off the water and petted his head.

"I'll get you something in a minute. I need to get my own breakfast started first."

No more thirteen dollar a pound coffee in their house. Not for months. She peeled off the lid to a cheap plastic coffee tub of the store brand Italian roast. If she had to opt for cheap coffee, it had better be strong.

The aroma of the coffee finally made Jackson begin to stir from his sleep on the couch. Farrah knew the couch was comfortable, but hell, it wasn't that comfortable. How he managed to be practically in a coma was beyond her understanding. Then again, maybe sleeping next to her was so undesirable that anywhere else in the world was a cozy paradise to him.

"Morning," he grumbled through a stretch.

"Morning."

Jackson swung his legs to the floor and looked down at the empty dog bed. Farrah returned to the kitchen to get almond milk from the refrigerator and a mug from a cabinet.

"Did you let Gordon out yet?"

"No. I just got down here."

"You could've let him out the back door before you started the coffee."

"Are you really going to start up with me less than a minute from waking up?"

Jackson put on the socks and sneakers that were on the floor next to the couch. He went to the dining room where Gordon greeted him with a low murmur in old dog speak for, *Jeez, man, you finally got your ass up so how about you take me out?*

He clipped the leash on the dog, grabbed his coat, and left through the dining room's door that lead to the driveway. Farrah hated this new phase of their morning routine. They had agreed on being amicable to each other when they sat down to acknowledge the proverbial rough patch.

The truce lasted about a week.

Farrah took her coffee back upstairs to continue packing. Miles was sound asleep in the suitcase where she left him.

"Come on, buddy. I love you, but this isn't helping Momma at all."

She tried poking him gently. He was a master at sleeping or at least pretending. Farrah put her heavy Polish ceramic mug on the nightstand and picked up the cat.

"Come. On. You. Loaf."

He purred.

"I win."

The cat stretched his back then immediately planted himself on one of the outfits laid out on the bed.

"Ok. You win."

There was never a point to battling with a cat. The cat's desires to shed on every article of clothing was a lifelong war she would never win.

Surveying the clothes, Farrah knew that she didn't have much more time to think about it. Packing her supplies for work was much more important than if she had the right socks to wear with khakis, polo shirts, and flannel. Not only had she never been on a business trip before, but she'd never been to any mountain retreat before for any reason.

Her massage supplies were neatly packed already in plastic bags inside a duffel bag. All the creams and essential oils were double bagged just in case of leakage because Farrah was paranoid enough over things going completely wrong. She had two packs of disposable face cradle covers, her lightest weight reference books, and a portable mp3 player loaded with serene new age music. Her laptop, chargers, forms and clipboards were packed in an attaché and ready to go.

She had no idea what to expect there. Fortunately, her boss from Riverside Wellness Spa was going to bring a van filled with all the linens and another massage therapist. Most of the other therapists couldn't take a week away from second jobs, families, or college classes.

Farrah wanted some time away home. It wasn't exactly her fantasy vacation, but they were told that after their appointments, their time was their own to enjoy all the amenities Shawnee Conference Center and Resort had to offer.

Miles didn't like it, but the clothes needed to go into the suitcase. It was time.

Farrah spent the next half hour packing snacks and energy drinks into a backpack. She tossed in an additional bottle of B-vitamins too. Hopefully, rejuvenation and vitality would come to her naturally from being around new faces, being inundated with work, and being a couple hundred miles from home.

She changed into a pair of cargo pants and a sweatshirt that was decorated with bouncy font spelling *Namasté*. She was going to keep trying to fool everyone else that she was an expert in relaxation. She was becoming a hell of an actress and hiding the truth about being a tense ball of anxiety.

"What are you doing?" Jackson came up behind her in the driveway while she loaded her bags into her Honda.

"What does it look like I'm doing? I'm loading my car."

"So you're leaving? Going to stay with your new lover June, I suppose?"

Farrah's face contorted from the combination of being stupefied and insulted.

"What? No! Stop ragging about me and June! She's my best friend and you know it! I'm packing for my business trip. You know - the one I told you about? The one where I will make more money in a week than I have this past six months? That's what the hell I'm doing."

Farrah slammed the trunk. Part of her wanted to resort to all kinds of name calling and vulgarities, but she wanted to be the one that tried to keep to their agreement of civility. It wasn't working well, but she felt like she earned more marriage points in her tally for fighting cleaner. Okay, so you were never supposed to think of marriage as having tallies, but once she and Jackson entered that He Did This/She Did That phase, it was hard not to.

A cell phone rang. The two of them locked eyes for a couple of seconds before realizing it was Jackson's phone inside his pocket.

"I suppose that's your new lover? Go on. Answer it. What difference does it make?"

The dog stood by his master's side without making a sound. He looked up at the humans and looked like he had a thousand thoughts running through his little canine brain.

Jackson took the phone out and said hello. Farrah shook her head and walked back into the house where Miles greeted her in the kitchen.

The cat jumped to the counter where he really shouldn't have been. Farrah gave him a kiss on the head and picked him up.

"Miles, what are we going to do?"

Her eyes began to burn, but she sniffed back any tears. She refocused her energy on the trip and the week ahead. Her new career hadn't been going particularly well, so there was no way she was going to let her personal life throw a monkey wrench into this trip. She needed to feed the cat, make sure his litter was clean, then do a final check on her own chores before leaving.

The cat was sated with cheap wet and dry food in his bowls. His water was topped off with ice cubes.

"All right, you. I'm sure you'll be fine without me for a few days." She ran her hand down his back and got some purring in return.

CHAPTER TWO

FARRAH heard the side door open and close then heard Gordon's nails clacking on the dining room floor. Walking the dog clearly didn't have a soothing effect on Jackson. After the passive-aggressive attitude he showed her already, she fully intended on saying nothing else to him until it was time for her leave. And even then, all she was willing to extend was a goodbye.

Jackson and Gordon returned to the kitchen. Farrah sat at the table with her head resting in her hands for a few moments. She listened to the sloppy sloshing of Gordon drinking water out of his bowl in the laundry room. Still no speaking. The refrigerator opened and closed as Jack got himself the water pitcher and filled a glass.

"It's right there," she said, "on the calendar."

"What?" He turned around.

"I have my trip marked on the calendar right there. It's

not like I was planning to abandon you. Though at this point, it seems it doesn't matter where I'm going."

He looked at the calendar with no particular interest. He wasn't studying it, only staring to avoid looking at her. Then he saw Thanksgiving weekend and the notations to pick up Janice at college.

"Are we really going to pretend to have a pleasant Thanksgiving and bring our daughter back home? She's not stupid. She'll know things are bad if I'm sleeping on the couch."

Farrah's look of contempt shot at him. She didn't care if they skipped the damn holidays all together, but she did miss her daughter. She wanted time to bond with her on an adult level now.

"Nova," she said.

"What?"

"She wants to be called Nova or did you forget that too? Janice legally changed her name, remember?"

"How could I forget? She erased my grandmother Margaret's legacy."

"I never liked Margaret as her middle name anyway." Farrah cringed when she realized that she reopened a twenty-year-old can of worms.

"I know."

Farrah waited to hear if he was going to continue with his

disappointment in family decisions or whether he'd want her to say something. He continued.

"There was nothing wrong with giving her a name from the black side of her family tree."

"I never said there was! I have never denied our daughter's right to understand her heritage!"

"Maybe you never realized it," he said. "You straightened her hair for how many years?"

"You're insane, Jack! I love our daughter. I took her to get her hair straightened when she asked for it. She wanted to fit in. She wanted to look like an actress from a show she watched. Not that you had any idea."

"She looks better now." His voice was quieter and sullen.

"She's beautiful. She's always been beautiful. She's the one thing we got right."

The argument was interrupted when his phone chimed from several notifications. More mysterious text messages.

Farrah rolled her eyes and shook her head. Only a month ago she was convinced he was having an affair with a woman from the town's committee to build a dog park. He went to a lot of "meetings" and "dinners" and his chat windows were always busy. Then he told her that the woman was a senior citizen and there was nothing to worry about. Farrah believed him and thought the whole thing had been a product of her anxiety and reading way too much into things.

"We need to come up with a plan. We need to figure this out. I thought things were going to get better after…" She trailed off.

"After you were cleared of murdering your client?"

"Yeah."

"Do you have any ideas?"

"What if we ask my mother to host this year since she's close to Moravian? It'd be easy to pick up… Nova… on the way, have dinner, and bring her back here."

"What if I don't want to spend the holiday with your mother and her boyfriend?"

"And me? What you really mean to say is, what if you don't want to spend the holiday with my family and me. Right? Do you have a suggestion?"

Farrah walked to the freezer and took out a frozen bagel. She popped it into the microwave for thirty seconds then put in the toaster. She gnashed and gnawed her way through the tension quite literally.

"We don't have to resolve this right now. You're leaving."

"For a business trip. My first business trip, by the way. And it's important to me like all your late night dinners and

Saturday meetings are to you. Anyway, I have an hour before I have to be on the road." She lost interest in her coffee specifically because it sucked. She craved a delicious cuppa, but even if she stopped for something at a cheap donut shop, that wasn't going to satisfy her.

"All I said was you're leaving and you're turning it into a confrontation."

She tried to defend her reply by explaining it was how he referred to her leaving. He had no position to be upset about her plans. He'd been living an active social life separate from her for a long time. And this was a professional week for her anyway. She would be busy with appointments and probably far too tired to enjoy herself. But, it seemed like he wasn't going to lay off the guilt trip.

"Look, unless you come up with a better plan for Thanksgiving, we'll go to my mother's. You don't have to come. I'm done trying to force you to spend time with your family. And we still are, by the way, me and my mother, and our daughter."

Her teeth tore into the bagel like a wild animal with its prey. She didn't care one bit if she spat while talking loudly. Being ladylike was a thing that was simply not going to be an achievement at that moment.

His phone chimed again. She stood still and watched him read the message. He toyed with her. He had to know she was sick with curiosity about who it was.

"Relax. It's Frank. He needs my help taking apart the haunted house stuff we spent four weeks putting together."

"Oh. Fine. Whatever. Tell him I said hello."

"Yeah I'm sure he wants to hear that. He's convinced June turned lesbian because of you."

Farrah let out a groan and slapped her palm on the counter barely missing the other bagel half.

"That's not how it works! The two of you need to quit this shit that June and I have been having this long lesbian affair that caused their divorce and has come between the two of us!"

"Oh please, Farrah, you admitted June hooked up with other women and that she has more than friendship feelings for you. We're not as stupid as you think."

It was another round of the same fight they've had a hundred times. Yes, her best friend once confessed to having deeper feelings for her, but they have remained platonic, sisterly, loving best friends just like before. June even went on a couple dates with a man, the manager of the local bar. Jed didn't seem that into June so she's still single and looking.

The good news was that Farrah knew her husband's style in not saying much in order to let her imagination run wild and give her theories far more destructive attention than reality. They hadn't been the sort of couple that fought much until the last couple years. He tended to redirect all his anger to her pansexual best friend, who admittedly took a lot of her attention.

It started with feelings of being distant and uninterested. The fighting didn't come until after Farrah lost her full-time job and became a massage therapist making almost no money for the household. She secretly wondered if he was jealous of her trying to build a new career out of nothing and being away from the daily grind in a cubicle. Because he had taken on all the expenses and they were scraping by, Farrah never wanted to talk to him about whether or not he wanted to make such a drastic change in his own professional life. She was afraid of the answer.

Jackson texted Frank back about being free all day so he could help dismantle the Halloween decorations, most of which Frank built himself. He didn't even look up when continuing the conversation.

"When I spent a few days at Frank's, it was good for us. We cooled off and then we were able to talk and behave like adults. You'll be gone all week. Everything here will be fine. I'm sure when you get back, our heads will be more clear. Right now though, I am honestly sick of this same fight too. There's no point in continuing until you get back."

"That's what I've been saying." Farrah threw the remainder of her bagel in the garbage, long since cold and unappealing.

Miles and Gordon congregated in the kitchen like the furry kids they were, wondering why Mommy and Daddy were always fighting. Miles was probably hoping that he'd get the house to himself again, but no such luck.

Farrah cleaned the litterbox once last time before she would have to trust Jackson to do it. She took out some cat treats and handfed them to Miles who had jumped on to his perch in the window.

She saw the old list of emergency contact numbers. Over the years, they had scribbled on new ones and crossed out old ones. June and Frank once had their own line with a single phone number. Now they were handwritten in with cell numbers. It wasn't because of the advances in technology either. It was a mundane reminder that a once happy couple was divorced. Farrah couldn't help but think the same future was destined for her.

A different series of blips and bloops snapped her out of her depressing thoughts. It was her phone's text messaging alert. She swiped the screen and panic immediately exploded inside her chest.

CHAPTER THREE

FARRAH saw the text message from Samantha and her hands began to shake as if the tightening in her chest wasn't enough to deal with. Samantha Waterston, the owner of Riverside Wellness Spa, was stuck in the Tampa airport watching the marquees change all the flight information to CANCELED because of an approaching tropical storm.

> FARRAH: What does this mean?
> Are you canceling the retreat?
>
> SAM SPA: No! You have to go.
> Christine will drive the van! I can't
> believe this!

Gordon didn't budge when Farrah accidentally stumbled into him. She paced without looking up from her phone so it was fortunate it was only the soft burly dog she collided into instead of hard furniture.

"Oh crap!"

Jackson reared his head in case it was something about him and asked what was wrong.

"Samantha is stuck in Florida and she still wants me and Christine to…"

Texts kept coming through rapidly delivering more bad news on top of the current crisis.

"No! No! No! No!"

"You can do it without her, right?"

"But now she's telling me that Christine can't make it either. She had to take her kid to the ER last night!"

"And don't you have nearly a dozen other massage therapists working in that spa?"

"But they can't do it. The three of us were the bare minimum. Other people have second jobs or full-time jobs or kids still at home. We were the only ones that could leave for a week. Crap!"

Farrah walked a couple more circles before plopping into a chair. Her fingertip pressed the green button on her screen to connect the call to her boss.

"I definitely can't do this by myself. There will be hundreds of people at that retreat."

She didn't want to sound hysterical to Samantha, but talking instead of texting seemed like a better option for the sake of speed and typos.

"I'm sorry, but we can't cancel. This is a huge opportunity for our business. For all of us. Caressa Lamour would be the most impressive client we have. Plus, they gave us a huge deposit that's already been spent on the extra linen service and van rental." Samantha's voice was loud, but not enough to completely drown out the background noise of other irate airline customers.

Farrah stewed over the quip that the deposit had already been spent. Sam owned the spa and each of the practitioners was an independent contractor so they had no say in the business decisions even though, according to the tax office, they were entrepreneurs.

"This is not a one-person job, Sam!"

"Can you bring someone to be your assistant? I'll pay them for their time of course."

Farrah couldn't believe what she just heard. Their biggest client, the most important series of appointments she's ever had and now she's supposed to do the entire job herself, alternating between big blocks of appointment times for chair and table massages.

She told her boss that she'd get back to her as soon as possible, but she needed to make some calls. Truthfully, there was only one person she wanted to call, June Cho.

"Hey, bitch, why are you calling me when I'm catching up on my shows?" Her Sunday routine was interrupted. June slurped her dark roasted Chemex brewed coffee. She recently kicked up her coffee snobbery an extra notch by investing in the fancy pot and figuring out how to use it.

A few weeks prior, June mentioned that she had to use up her vacation days before the year was up or lose them. She worked for the county clerk in the department that handled things like deeds and property records. Besides being the one person to always bail Farrah out, literally and figuratively, she would be the one person who could take time off and go with her since her only other option was her daughter still at school.

Farrah explained her trouble. It was enough to get June to pause her TV at a critical scene where one of the show's stars was about to leap off a roof to her death.

"Let me message my boss. I'm sure she's up by now even on a Sunday."

"Thank you so much. I don't know what I'd do without you."

"Without me? You'd be rotting in jail. You'd be doing someone else's hair in the yard on recess."

"Don't remind me." Farrah sat quietly instead of venting further to her husband.

It only took a few minutes before June called back and said she had no problem taking the week off. She was lucky because the following week was a major convention for the municipal and county clerks, mayors, and other politicians in Atlantic City. She'd have to be back at the office picking up the slack by then.

Farrah was still sitting in the chair in the dining room. Jackson relocated to the living room with the TV on where the local meteorologist talked about the temperatures being ten degrees below normal.

From the other room, Farrah raised her voice to update him on the latest news. "I guess I'm still going."

She tried to read his expression when he looked up. She saw that his facial muscles were far more relaxed than half an hour ago as were his normally tense shoulders.

She walked to the threshold between the rooms. "Do you even care?"

"Yes, I care. I'm glad you can still go and do your thing. You'll be fine."

"June's going with me to help out. She'll help me carry everything and be in charge of the appointment book. She's using her vacation days to go to work for me."

Part of Farrah wanted Jackson to speak up and tell her that she should tell June to forget it and that he would go instead - that he would take off those days to support her new career from the frontline. He was supportive behind the scenes by taking on all the burden of their finances, but so many of their discussions made Farrah feel like he thought her job was meaningless. He never agreed with half her education that focused on non-Western medicine. To him, some of the therapies were frivolous witch doctor scams.

This trip, though, this would be Farrah's big chance to work on corporate professionals just like him. People who were overworked, spent far too much of their lives behind desks, and whose efforts to have better health were always brushed aside after failing at New Year's resolutions, opting for the speed and efficiency of whatever was most convenient. It was the sort of assignment Jackson should have supported.

"This retreat center seems really nice too. Maybe it's something your office should look into. They have a bunch of activities for groups that are supposed to help people reconnect and improve communication. Ya know, things where you support each other? Like trust exercises and helping someone over a big wall."

He wasn't biting or reading into it that she meant it would be good for them not his coworkers.

"Wharton and Finkle would never spend the money."

It was time for her to head out. There was no kiss. He at least said goodbye and good luck. Farrah accepted that it had to be enough and felt wrong for expecting more. She drove to June's condo a mile away. They wouldn't be able to simply load up the car and leave either.

It took a while for June to pack so Farrah was getting a much later start than she wanted, but the bonus was having better coffee. The trip would be further delayed by all the other hurdles that were now in her path. They weren't going to take Farrah's car or even June's SUV. They had to go pick up the rental van then the linens. Before they could do that, Farrah unpacked her laptop and booted it up to show June the software used to manage her schedule.

"Most of the stuff we normally use in the office you won't be going into. We won't be taking down medical histories or recording details of the sessions. All we really need done are to have the forms signed saying they aren't knowingly getting a massage if they have a contraindication condition - which don't worry, I'll ask them again anyway - and then we need to have the sessions logged to prove how many clients were seen."

She showed June how there was a dedicated project set up with the customer name: Caressa Lamour Cosmetics. If everything worked properly, big "if," the paper files would only be for backup. Each person was expected to read through the document and electronically sign their agreement to the terms. The software would link the signature to the log of appointments. Every two hours, the files were set to automatically back up to a security-compliant cloud server.

"Seems easy enough." June gave Farrah a pat on the shoulder hoping to ease her anxiety.

"It seems easy. I mean, the steps to enter the information are easy. But what worries me is the sheer number of people we'll be seeing. I've never worked on that many people before. I've never had a schedule like this."

"Don't worry. I will insist that you have scheduled breaks because I know you. You'll keep going because you don't want to turn anyone away."

"I know. It's important that I don't hurt myself. I'll need breaks."

"But… admit it, you're likely to push through. Not eating. Not resting. Not going to the bathroom. Afraid that if someone sees you sitting down for five minutes they'll judge you for not working hard enough."

Farrah knew June was right. She had issues with guilt even though she was the type of practitioner to lecture her clients in the importance of rest and play away from their work spaces.

CHAPTER FOUR

THEY filled up Farrah's small sedan and drove thirty minutes to the rental car place. The small highway with traffic lights every quarter mile or less added to the straws mounting on her back. One of them, she feared, would be the final one.

Do not pass out from the stress. Do not pass out from the stress. Do not pass out from the stress.

Farrah made her worrying worse when she commanded herself to calm down and reminded herself that operating a car while passed out from anxiety would make many people's day suck, not only her own.

The powers of the universe continued to screw with her.

"What do you mean you don't have our van? My boss reserved one and then she called to inform you that I'd be the one signing it out instead of her."

Farrah wanted to keep herself in check when she talked to the rental clerk. She tried. She failed. Any semblance of cool demeanor was out the door.

"I'm sorry, but according to the computer, this reservation was canceled. We don't really change the reservation names. So, like… what we have to do is cancel them and open a new ticket."

"Okay. Mike, is it?" His name tag was free from scars and wear, probably new. "Mike, I understand that reservation number was canceled. There should be a new reservation with my name."

"Hmmm. I don't see anything."

June slid her aviator glasses down the bridge of her nose. She looked like one of those TV cops that had a past life a supermodel before going into a dedicated life of law enforcement. It was a clear message: do not mess with her.

"Hey there, Mike. Listen, here's the thing. Out there in your parking lot, you have like six or seven vehicles just sitting there. One of them is a van. The van we want. The van we need. You want to give us what we need, don't you? Can't you rent us that van since the person who originally wanted it canceled?"

"Oh. Um. Let me check." Mike tapped away at the computer terminal. His brow furrowed like he was breaking into the Pentagon.

After a few minutes, June's patience was burning out. She slapped her hand on the counter and jolted Mike out of his concentration.

"Hey! Give us that van! That one right over there! We're here. We have a credit card. We're trying to give you business. Why is this so goddamn difficult?"

"Jeez, lady. Okay."

He walked to a back office and intentionally wasted time pretending to locate the keys they needed. He dangled them from his fingers but pulled back quickly when June reached for them.

"Now, how about that insurance?"

Ten minutes later, the ladies were driving the van and Farrah's car back to the spa which was closer than her house.

"Sam said the bags of linens would be stored in Room One so no one would confuse them with the ones in the storage room." Farrah pushed the buttons in sequence to unlock the office condo's back door.

They tried to be as quiet as possible walking through the long hallway. The serene music was piped through all the rooms. The wall sconces were dimmed to a warm, ambient light. A couple of the doors were closed which meant people were in session. Room Three wasn't. It was wide open and the light inside was dimmed to near darkness.

"This is where it happened," Farrah whispered to June. "Where Walter Koczak died on my table."

June gently touched Farrah's shoulder. "I'm sorry, sweetie. Let's get the bags and get out of here as fast as possible, okay?"

They made two trips back and forth to the van. They followed Samantha's instructions and only took half of the linens that had been delivered. With Farrah being the only massage therapist able to take appointments, there's no way she could cover the same number as three of them.

"Do we need anything else from here?"

"No, I don't think so. I'm bringing my own music and we use our own creams and oils. I'm cutting out any frills. No hot stones or cold marble. Screw that. I'll be crazy as it is."

"Looks like we need to stop to fill the tank of this beast." June petted the van like it was an oversized dog.

"Well, I wish I had the company credit card, but I have my own. I guess I'll just use it and add it to the expense list to invoice the spa when we get back. Sam said she'd reimburse me for everything."

"And she's paying me, right?"

"Yes. She swore she would. Instead of three therapists and an assistant being paid, it's just me and you, so that's money she'll shell out anyway." Farrah did a cursory double-check of the supplies in the back.

"I'm sure the corporation hiring you isn't going to pay for all four now, are they?"

"I doubt it, but I'm not about to get involved in the spa's finances. I'm bad enough keeping my own straight. I'm still not in the black."

They left Farrah's car at the office park. She popped herself into the van's driver seat. June set her phone's GPS navigation and off they went. They made a quick stop while still near town to gas up.

"Did you bring any other CDs besides the new age stuff?"

"No. Did you?"

"No. And this thing is apparently too bare bones to have a Bluetooth setup, so no podcasts or anything from my phone either."

"Gee, I guess we'll just have to talk to each other for two hours. How awful!"

June turned on the radio anyway and they were in range of the one decent country station that came in clear.

"I know how I'm going to spend the next two hours while you drive."

"How's that?"

"I'm going to finally set you up with professional social

media accounts so I can post to them this whole week. What kinds of things do your coworkers post?"

"I don't know. I hardly look at that stuff."

"You're not hopeless, Farrah. I refuse to believe you are that hopeless. I'm not saying it isn't good to unplug for a while, but you have the kind of job that isn't plugged in all day long, so your non-work time can be spent online. It's good promotion and networking. You'll see."

"God, June. You talk to me like I'm a dinosaur. I know what social media is. I know how to use it. I simply choose not to be glued to it until my eyeballs dry out."

Another half an hour went by before June spoke. She was the type of person glued to social media and her eyes never popped out. She probably needed new glasses and stock in eye drops from all the scrolling. Her day job was boring as hell. She got her work done as expected so if that meant she could waste a third of her day checking on the latest news or outrage, that's what she did.

"Hmmm, so here's the thing…" Whenever June started a sentence with *here's the thing*, it usually meant she was about to go off like she did with the dumb rental car guy.

"What?"

"It pretty much looks like anyone with the word massage in their bio is really a hooker. I mean, I'm assuming you wouldn't normally advertise with an avatar with giant boobs in a lace bra or a G-string?"

"Yeah, please no. I don't want my avatars to be me naked. No one needs that and I certainly don't want those clients."

"Do you have a cool picture of you working wearing the scrubs or something like that? Like you'd see in a medical brochure?"

"No. Just find a stock photo of candles and stones or whatever. The Riverside brochures and website have some nice ones. We're allowed to use her graphics in our materials."

"Good enough for me. You can even use the business logo, right? That's part of your working arrangement?"

"Oh definitely. My business cards are the same design as Sam and Maggie's. I do have licensed images from my professional network, but they're on a disk back home."

June said she would snap as many photos as possible of Farrah working, of course, only after getting the permission of anyone seen in the images. Plus, it would only be the sessions where clients were fully clothed. She volunteered herself to be the toweled model in other shots if they could recruit someone to take the pictures.

The trip through western New Jersey was lush with gorgeous fall foliage in bright reds, orange, and gold. As far as road trips went, this one was pretty lovely. The GPS said they had about twenty miles remaining to get to the Shawnee Conference Center and Resort just shy of the Pennsylvania border. It was only supposed to be a few minutes from when they could unpack and enjoy their Sunday afternoon before the chaos of the work week began the next day.

"Oh my god! What is that?" Farrah said. "What's happening?"

CHAPTER FIVE

THE car lost power and Farrah had enough sense to check her mirrors in a matter of seconds to make sure no one was barreling down on them. She glided the car to the shoulder. Her foot was on the brake so hard, it practically brought her to standing.

"What the hell!" June said.

"I don't know. It just stopped. I didn't do anything."

"Shit! Do you have triple-A?"

"No. I canceled anything that didn't seem critical. I don't suppose the rental agreement covers roadside assistance. Can you get that out and check?"

June pulled the copy of the contract from her purse. There was nothing useful in the tiny print. She suggested that Farrah call the rental agency anyway and ask them what to do.

Farrah ground her teeth and a guttural sound escaped through them. She tossed her phone on to the dashboard cubby hole.

"He said they don't cover roadside assistance. That little shit! I'll be emailing his boss."

"Girl, please. He's a teenager who doesn't care about his weekend job. I'm blaming your boss for this one. She could've used a reputable name brand rental agency instead of some skeevy-looking lot of decrepit cars."

Farrah agreed. Blaming Sam felt really good at that moment. It was Sam who booked this job. Sam who got stuck in Florida during a tropical storm. Sam who made the reservation for a rundown old van.

"Let's get out and look under the hood. Maybe we'll see something," Farrah said.

"Do you know anything about cars?"

"Very little, but hopefully enough to describe the problem to Jackson when I inevitably call him to save our asses."

Farrah released the hood's latch from the inside. The women exited the vehicle while other cars slowed down to rubberneck. People gawked and since there was no sign of injury, no wounded animal, no crumpled parts of the van, they had better things to do than stop and ask if the women needed help.

"Nothing is smoking so that's good, I guess," Farrah said.

"Do you have any tools or even a flashlight for seeing in there?" June said.

"There's got to be some tools for changing a tire under the carpeting. I don't have a flashlight though." Farrah started to resign herself to the fate being helpless.

"Wait. Let me get my phone. I know there are flashlight apps you can download. I saw people talk about it during Superstorm Sandy."

"You and that phone. I swear if you manage to get us out of this, I'll never mock you again for how addicted you are to that thing."

They walked to back of the Ford Windstar and opened the creaking doors. All the bags filled with the pristine linens, their luggage, a massage table, and a massage chair were unloaded and lined up on the side of the road in a shoulder filled with browning red oak leaves past their prime.

"You said you wanted to see the fall foliage after Halloween, right?" Farrah said.

"Not this way. It looks like we missed the peak weeks up here. We should've broken down two weeks ago," June said. "Any idea where we are exactly?"

"Other than 202, not really. I think the last sign I saw was for Sterling. The lake isn't far, but the retreat center is on the far side of it from where we are.

"Why did we take this route? That seems like it brought us out of our way?" June said.

"I don't know. I was relying on your GPS."

Farrah pulled back the carpet and found the spare tire and some tools. She hoped that it would be enough to get them going once they could diagnosis the problem.

"Oh, hey, what's that?" June wasn't looking in the back of the van. She faced the road behind them and pointed to something in the middle of the lane.

"I don't know. Go see, but be careful. It could be a snake."

June walked there and back. She returned with a long black thing in her hand. It was the serpentine belt.

"I kind of wish it would've been a snake," June said.

"At least now we know what's wrong."

"Any idea how to fix it?"

"Let me think."

They went back to the front of the van and peered into the dark abyss of the engine. June lit up the cell phone app which didn't do a great job of illuminating anything since it was still daylight out.

"You know what? I have much better use for that thing. Although I was impressed that you thought of a flashlight app. Look up videos on repairing this belt."

They sat through a fifteen-minute tutorial of two mechanics replacing a belt on the exact model van. Of course they had a proper garage, safety gear, tools, and the knowledge of what they were doing.

"This doesn't help, Farrah. Even if we have all the tools, we don't have a replacement belt no less those things they talked about like pulleys."

"I don't want to call Jackson. I really don't. We are not in a good place where I feel like asking him to save us. He's still got it in his head that you and I are having an affair behind his back. So does your ex-husband, by the way."

"What else can we do?"

They sat on the back end of the van and no other cars came by. Farrah took the belt from June's hand and stared it. She inspected the weathering. There were cracks all over it. It obviously should've been replaced months ago. Chances are, no one had signed out that van for quite some time; or maybe they had, but got lucky. She took the two broken ends and pieced them together, holding it in place to see the size of the loop it made. She continued to be mesmerized by the rubber loop until June snapped her out of it.

"What are you doing?"

"I have an idea." Farrah popped off the tail end and darted to her luggage.

"What are you doing? Are you going to tell me?"

Farrah unzipped her attaché case and began pulling out

all her device chargers. She set aside the plugs with large heavy power units. The other plugs were straightened and laid next to each other. She put the broken belt next to them and saw that two charger cords were just a little bit longer than the belt.

"I think if we can tie these together and string them properly through the pulleys, it might be enough to get us to a gas station!"

"What?" June was flabbergasted. The idea was so preposterous that it stood a chance of working.

"I guess it's finally paying off that I tend to forget to pack my chargers, so I keep buying them. The laptop one won't work, but these for phones and file transfers, they should work. We just have tie them as tight as possible, so they stay knotted."

They went back to the engine and tried to identify where the parts were that the mechanics in the video talked about. The video instructions pointed out that reaching the pulley would be difficult and that they would need to remove the tire from the passenger side of the van.

"Get the jack. I'll get the wrenches," Farrah told June.

Together they slid underneath the van and hoped the spot they picked for the jack was the safest bet.

"I can't get these lug nuts to budge," Farrah said.

They took turns trying to move the ratchet and socket. The lugs must have been put on with an air gun. It took all their strength and determination to loosen them. June even jumped on the ratchet as hard as she could to get the most stubborn nut to give way. Finally, June lifted the car without any problem.

"We don't have anything to replace that tensioner though," June said.

"Who cares at this point? All we need to do is get moving. It might be slowly, but we'll get moving and get to a garage where professionals can fix the damn thing properly. And while they're doing that, I'll call Samantha and tell her this trip is a goddamn disaster and that she's going to be getting this bill in with my invoice of expenses."

To tighten the knots of the charger cords, they basically played a game of tug-a-rope, each pulling an end as hard as they possibly could. When making the final knot to enclose the loop, they pulled again on the rubbery circle they made and all the knots tightened.

It took a lot of cursing and scraping of skin for them to squeeze their hands through the engine components. June was underneath passing the loop up to Farrah who forced it around the alternator.

Farrah let out a warrior yell while pulling to fit the loop around the last pulley. It looked like it would be tight enough to stay without slipping off the side.

"Fingers crossed," June said.

Farrah turned the key and the engine came back to life. June used the phone's GPS to find the closest garage which they prayed would be open on a Sunday. All they needed was to get five miles up the road. They loaded up the equipment and luggage in a bit of a careless manner and got back into their seats.

Farrah's grip on the steering wheel was so tight, her hands changed color. Every quarter mile, she muttered about how much further they had to go. June kept announcing the countdown of their ETA. Four and a half miles. Four miles. Three and a half. Three. Until they saw the Mecca that was Bo's Oil and Service on the left-hand side of the road.

"I can't believe we made it," Farrah said.

"I hope that retreat center has bourbon."

"They better. And I'm sure as hell going to expense that to Samantha too."

The mechanic at Bo's garage had plenty of pity for the ladies and their broken van. It wasn't Bo himself. June and Farrah whispered about whether Bo was a real person or some kind of backwater New Jersey legend. Maybe the real Bo wasn't a modern mechanic, but rather a heroic Colonial man who rescued people from the roadside when their carriage wheels snapped on the rocky mountain terrain. His name was Beauregard Longshanks, but the folks in these parts called him Bo. Everyone knew him and he knew them.

Farrah and June managed to keep themselves entertained and laughed instead of cry. The mechanic had to run out for parts, but after a few hours, everything was patched up.

"I want to bail on this crap. I want to turn this piece of shit around and go right back home," Farrah said.

"Can you? Do you think Samantha would understand by this point after everything we've gone through?"

Farrah knew exactly what Samantha would say. That woman wouldn't give up business for anything. Clearly the threat of her being washed away by a hurricane was proof that she would manage to find a way to give orders so the office could continue to run.

"Look, I know this a bad start of epic proportions, but I'm here to help you. If you want to turn around, that's fine by me. We can stop for what might be an expensive dinner out here. Or, we could pull out of this parking lot, get to the retreat center, and unpack all this. And then, we will figure out where we're staying and order room service, if that exists. If it doesn't, we'll find something that delivers."

"Do you see where we are? We're in the middle of nowhere," Farrah said.

"They'll have pizza. Every town has pizza."

"It's Podunk City in County Nowhere. They are not known for their pizza here."

"But they also have liquor. We'll stop on the way and get a bottle of whatever you want. We'll drink enough that even terrible pizza can be washed down."

Farrah chuckled and said that plan sounded vile, but she didn't have any other suggestions. She made a left and steered them north up a small highway then east to the lake. No critters jumped out in front of them. They didn't hit any potholes. It was a pleasantly uneventful last few miles.

CHAPTER SIX

IT seemed like nothing short of a miracle that the road was paved. There was one street light as sad and lonely as the asphalt. The dismal service road lead them to the main building. Its rustic wooden slats might have been warm and welcoming during the day, but the early sunset of November made Farrah feel like an axe murderer was waiting for them. Maybe not an axe. Maybe a chainsaw. Either way, she did not get the sense of cozy wonder the Shawnee Conference Center website promised.

"You don't have to go less than one mile an hour. The van is fixed."

"It's fixed, but the van and I want to turn around and run. Look at this place!"

Farrah rode the brake and allowed the van to creep across the crunchy asphalt. There were several rows of parked cars close to the building. Farrah tried to look for an empty space, but her eyes betrayed her and kept focusing on the building.

"Over there." June spotted the signs indicating there was more parking down a narrow road and one for a loading area down a small incline to the side of the monstrous building.

"Maybe we should go into the lobby first to ask where exactly we need to set up and get keys for our room," Farrah said.

"I hope the showers are the kind with jet sprayers on all sides. I just want to lean up against that and…"

"Stop! Just stop! I don't need to hear this right now."

"Oh, please. Tell me you never enjoyed the variable settings of that massaging shower head you installed."

"It's for my shoulder tension!"

"Uh huh."

They pulled up to the portico in the front of the building and left the van there. Inside, the bright lights jarred them back from the horror movie setting that initially greeted them. The registration table for the Caressa Lamour conference was the first point of arrival, but no one was there. The official conference center check-in desk was to the left at the back of a gorgeous lobby which took its log cabin chic design seriously.

The clerks at the desk wore denim or flannel shirts instead of the usual dark blazers of hotel chains. A woman with long dark hair noticed Farrah and June as they approached.

"Yes, we have a note here that Samantha Waterston called

and explained there would be some alterations in your plan," Cynthia the clerk said. "Your party was set up in a suite with four rooms and a common living/dining area. We're fully booked, so there's unfortunately no way to change both of you to a smaller accommodation."

Farrah asked if they would still be able to put the charges through to Samantha's card or if she needed to be here. Cynthia said their suite was already incorporated into the booking reservation for the Caressa Lamour staff so, fortunately, Farrah wouldn't have to worry about adding that to her own credit card.

They got their key cards and decided to unload the massage gear before taking their luggage to their suite. Bob from the maintenance department met them at the loading area on the side of the building. They put the bags of the linens and all the gear onto a flatbed trolley. Bob wheeled it for them to the suite set up specifically for their work.

The first room had a small loveseat, a desk with a phone, and lamps. In the room that normally housed an oval conference table, it was mostly empty for Farrah to set up the massage table. She stored the massage chair there too, because it would be used out in the public space of the conference center.

She assessed the mood of the room to see how it compared to her space the spa. The room lights were on a dimmer which would make up for her lack of ambient flameless candles or salt lamps. Once people's eyes were closed and they could only hear soft peaceful music, they would forget they were in a conference room.

"If you need help with your personal luggage, I can take that to your room for you too," Bob said.

"That would be nice. Thank you," Farrah said.

"Since we are getting here later than expected, do you know what there is for us to do? We hoped to unwind before a jam packed work week," June said.

"Well, you're not all that late really. I was still helping the makeup people get to their rooms a half an hour ago." Bob walked over to a credenza and picked up a print out that was next to a notebook of the activities and amenities offered. "Here's the program of the main events. It's my understanding these are the things for everyone. Then there's a programming schedule for small group activities. But, here you can see when meals are and their presentations and things like that."

After Bob got them to their own suite, June went with Farrah to park the van in one of the additional lots so that she wouldn't have to walk in the dark alone. Even if Farrah embraced the flashlight app, she knew that creepy feeling would stick with her walking along the narrow road encased by the tall shedding trees.

"Are you going to let Jackson know you got here relatively safely?"

Farrah looked straight ahead while she thought about June's question. "Nope. He doesn't care."

"I doubt that's true. I'm sure he cares if you're injured or dead."

"You've never been one to advocate for him before. What's up with that?"

"I don't know. Part of me loves when it's just you and me and we're off doing our *Thelma and Louise* thing. But, I know you love him and I hate seeing you hurt every single day."

Hurting every day definitely sucked. It was hard for Farrah to come to terms with how terrible she felt. She felt like a fraud, a charlatan. It'd be like if it was a discovered a diet guru actually had liposuction. She thought someday her clients would discover her secret that she can't get relaxation techniques to work for her and there's no real thing as stress management despite all the stuff she preached.

June grabbed Farrah's arm and forced her to stop walking.

"Did you hear that?"

"Don't play games, June. Let's get back inside and figure out where to find food."

"Shh! No. Listen!"

They couldn't see where the voices came from. They

were close to a break in the trees that overlooked the lake and part of the trails.

"Stay quiet," June said. "Come over here. Maybe we can see something."

"Should we really be snooping like this? People are talking. So what?"

Then Farrah realized how angry the male voices sounded.

"You can't release that to the public! Do you have any idea what that will do?" one said.

"It's the ethical thing to do," the other said.

"And where's the ethics in creating a storm that will put hundreds, if not thousands, of people out of work?"

June crouched down to peer around a tree. She grabbed Farrah and tugged her to get down too. Farrah slapped her hand away. Doing so, she didn't watch the ground underneath and her foot snapped a twig.

"What was that?" one man said.

"I'm out of here. But we're not finished with this. I'll see it to."

The men dispersed without discovering the women spying on them.

"I can't believe you. Don't you know how to eavesdrop?"

"I can't believe you think eavesdropping on strangers who are paying us is a good idea!"

"Oh my god. Let's get out of here."

"That's what I've been trying to do!"

When they entered the building, there was a woman by herself at the registration table.

"Oh, hi. We tried to register before, but no one was here," Farrah said.

"I'm so sorry. We were supposed to close the registration at six, but there have been all kinds of travel delays because of that tropical storm. I was assigned to take over for the folks who were doing it. I'm Mary Woodson, Milton Byron's assistant."

Farrah explained about the changes in their plans while Mary Woodson looked through a bin of envelopes.

"Here we are. Farrah Wethers, a badge for you and here's your information packet with the programming guide. I'm sorry, Ms. Cho, we don't have a badge with your name on it, but let me dig around and see if I can find a blank one."

It took about five minutes of patience that neither one of them seemed to have left after their ridiculous day of unfortunate events. Eventually, Mary found a blank badge, wrote June's name on it, and ran it through the laminating machine to her right.

They would need to present their key cards and access badges for anything they attended including the meals.

"Um, I know it's late, but is there any way we can still get food?"

"Oh sure. They have a restaurant right down there. You can just put it all on your room. I think they'll keep the kitchen open late for us. But, honestly, you don't want to miss the opening ceremonies. They're at ten o'clock and we have a couple stand-up comedians to start off the conference. And there will be some desserts and coffee there."

"Desserts?" June was finally paying attention.

"Okay, thank you, Mary. We'll hit the restaurant first."

The restaurant was like the lobby. Wood from floor to ceiling, a couple of heads mounted on the wall of formerly majestic creatures, and the furniture was upholstered in plaid. A few tables away and along the wall were a couple of men talking over drinks. The one wearing a suit was drinking a Manhattan; the other's beer accessorized his casual khakis and button down shirt sans tie.

June mulled over the menu, undecided by how good all the descriptions sounded. Farrah's vegetarian diet had hardly anything to choose from other than some pasta and salad. It would have to do. Unfortunately, it would probably have to do all week long for two meals a day, if she was even able to get that many breaks.

"What are you...?" Farrah began to say.

"Shhhhh!" June furrowed her brow and lowered her head to sink it further into the menu.

"What?"

"I'm listening. To them." She thrust her head in a micro gesture towards the men with the drinks.

"What is your problem tonight? Why are you eavesdropping on everyone?"

"Because when we sat down, one of the voices over there sounded familiar like one of the voices outside. And that one guy in the suit could match the one silhouette we saw arguing."

Farrah glanced over at them and tried not to look like she was swiveling around specifically to look at them.

"Even if he is, it's none of our business."

"You heard what I did, sweetie. The second someone mentions job loss, it's newsworthy and gossip-worthy and tweet-worthy."

"Don't you dare spread unfounded rumors online!" Farrah kept her voice low yet firm enough to come across matronly.

"I wouldn't dream of it, but I do love to be in-the-know, especially hearing it before anyone else."

"June, after I lost my job and I'm sitting here right in front of you, how can you make light of this?"

"I'm sorry, sweetie. I will feel bad for all those people.

Not nearly as bad as I did for you, but you're making me sound like a callous monster. I think this economy blows! Even rumors of layoffs affect the market."

Farrah did not share June's enthusiasm for the possible breaking news story. She ate her spaghetti marinara in nearly complete silence. Then she suggested they get out of their filthy clothes that they wore to fix the van and get ready in time for the entertainment at the opening ceremonies.

CHAPTER SEVEN

MONDAY

FARRAH was showered and dressed long before she needed to be. The suite Caressa Lamour provided for them was so large, she and June had their own bathrooms. It was heavenly. Not that June was the high maintenance type to fill a vanity with a hundred different eye shadows, hair spray, and irons. June was pretty basic like Farrah. Although after twenty years of sharing space with a family, Farrah reveled in every bit of personal sanctuary she could experience.

The outside door of the suite opened and closed. Farrah was momentarily frightened and peered her head out the door of her bedroom. Rustling noises were heard. She hoped the maid service wasn't ridiculously early.

"You're finally up. Come get breakfast." June had laid

out a spread of scrambled eggs, pancakes, juice, coffee, and grapes. "Come on! You need to load up if you expect to have energy to last you until lunchtime."

The enormous grin from the shock was all Farrah had to repay June for the feast. Plus, it was a breakfast feast - Farrah's favorite meal of the day.

"I cannot believe you got out of bed earlier than you do for work in order to find us breakfast. You're the best! And now I want to cry because I don't know how I can even face a full day of clients. I want to stay in here and hide and eat. Can we do that?"

June smirked and pulled the laptop over to the small round table that served as their eating nook. She swiveled it around to show Farrah the neurotically organized schedule that was set so far.

"Of course, there will be changes as we go along. There are always going to be late people or cancellations or people begging to be fit in at a time that's already booked. Just like a doctor. So are you okay with being flexible?"

Farrah's response through a mouthful of pancakes was unsure yet leaning towards positive. "Mrigushso."

"You guess so? Come on, soldier. Where's that enthusiastic mountain warrior spirit?"

"Mwrilosit."

"You did not lose it. You haven't started yet. You know they have some morning yoga for those corporate people to get them to start their day? This setup is wild. They'll be hiking and rock climbing. How the heck does this count as work for them?"

Farrah washed down her food with some coffee noting that they were not going to get almond milk unless they remembered to request it.

"It's for team building. I'm not really sure. I'm curious if they make everyone attempt these things. Plenty of people aren't that physically active."

"I read through this whole binder before going to sleep. They have low impact choices that involve drawing, puzzles, word games and more crafty types of things. They couldn't possible expect 60-year-old Mary to climb ropes. I mean, it's not the number, but it looks like she's aged like an average person not an athlete."

Farrah wanted to answer June, but it took her several seconds to decide whether to have another scoop of eggs and a pancake. What the hell? She'd burn it off later. She dove in and continued talking.

"It sounds fun. I can't believe companies shell out for a week of this. Those comedians last night were pretty good too."

"Especially the second guy. Pretty sure I saw him on Cracked."

"What's that? Ya know, never mind. I'm used to not knowing what you're talking about."

"Jeez, Farrah, you sound older than Mary. You can be such a Luddite."

"I'm not! I've embraced the internet. I let you set up all those pages and accounts for me. By the way, how's that going? What have I allegedly said?"

June toggled to the browser and showed Farrah the feeds she created. She already made some general announcements about being at the lodge for Caressa Lamour and tagged the corporation formally so their followers would see it.

"Okay, well, I can't think about all that right now. You handle it. Just don't say anything political or that could get me sued."

Farrah's first appointment times were for full body massages in the suite they set up the night before. She had four in a row. She was lucky if she got assigned four in a week at Riverside Wellness Spa.

They each grabbed books and personal items Farrah hadn't left in the treatment room and walked through the quiet hallway. They arrived at the much louder lobby to find it filled with Caressa Lamour employees dressed in sportswear or casual clothes, each one wearing an identification badge.

"They don't look like they're socializing," June said.

"What are they looking at?"

Through the enormous bank of windows, a flock of protesters could be seen. Their chants and yells were loud enough to penetrate the murmurs of the assembled employees.

"This is one way to start the celebration for reaching our sales goals." A man next to Farrah leaned towards her and spoke none too quietly.

"What's going on?" She continued to stare like everyone else.

"They're animal rights activists," he said.

Farrah leaned over to fill June in on the disturbance. June immediately took out her phone to see if there was anything online trending about Caressa Lamour.

"I'm Derek." The man extended his hand. "Derek Davis. And you're not one of us, are you?"

"Not officially. I'm Farrah Wethers, the massage therapist hired for this week."

She wondered why she had a strange feeling. She felt his smile, actually felt it, directed towards her like a breeze gently blowing in her face. It's not that Derek's features were mesmerizing Farrah exactly. It was his demeanor and friendliness which weren't over exaggerated or phony like so many people that end up in corporate sales. Farrah always found them obnoxious, loud, and pretentious in how they tried so hard to be the center of attention instead of presenting whatever product they were selling.

"Does this sort of thing happen a lot?" she said.

"The protests? Never before. Not with us anyway. Our brand specifically says it's cruelty-free on the labels."

"Farrah, take a look at this." June passed the phone to her.

On the trending hashtag, there was a link to BARN, Benevolent Animal Rights Network. They claimed Caressa Lamour had been covering up animal testing for years. Farrah opened the link, but the post didn't provide much information at all. It said that someone infiltrated the company and shot video proving the claim, but that the activists would give Caressa Lamour twenty-fours to come clean before the damaging evidence is posted publicly.

"They're eco-terrorists," Derek said.

June nudged Farrah to check out a man who walked to the front of the herd in the lobby. Farrah decided to pry what more she could from her new friend Derek.

"Hey, who's that?"

"That's our CEO, Milton Byron. And that guy walking behind him is Brad Dubray, the vice-president of the skincare division. He's always up Milton's ass like that."

Farrah and June exchanged looks. They recognized the older man as the one they saw having drinks the night before.

Brad Dubray wasn't the other man with him at that time though.

"This is really blowing up the internet." June took the phone back from Farrah.

Milton Byron raised his hands up to get the employees to quiet down. The protests outside grew louder. Farrah could read some of the signs that were everything from slogans to photos of real animals being tortured.

"I have already talked on the phone with Markos Demisovski, the conference center's highest security contractor. He'll be arriving as soon as possible, as will the local police. They'll remove these people from the conference center property."

He continued to assure them that they were completely safe and there was nothing to worry about. It took another fifteen minutes before the police arrived and dispersed the crowd. Two people were arrested, or at least put in handcuffs and put in the back of squad cars. Who knows - maybe they wouldn't be charged, but the cops wanted to control rowdy and unpredictable people.

The ones who would have been instructed to leave of their own accord had clearly left their personal vehicles off the property. The police had to make several trips back and forth to unload them somewhere which left only one officer to keep tabs on the crowd. State police showed up, and in a short amount time, it looked like they were evenly matched.

The cosmetic company's employees were urged to make their way to their first scheduled event. However, Milton Byron, Brad Dubray, a couple other Caressa Lamour executives, and representatives from the conference center went outside to talk to the police.

"I am going to be sick if this is true," one woman in the crowd said as she walked within earshot of Farrah.

"What if they're right? What does that mean?" said another.

"...not losing my job over this..." was uttered more than once by several people.

If ever there was a stressed out crowd that needed relaxing massages, Farrah found it.

"Well, Derek, it was nice to meet you." Farrah shook his hand again and started to leave.

"I guess I'll be seeing you tomorrow. I actually have an appointment with you. It's good to know I'll be in capable hands."

Her nerves flip-flopped in her stomach. "Uh. Okay then. See you tomorrow or later or whatever."

June nudged her. "You're babbling. What the hell is wrong with you?"

"I have no idea."

Farrah pivoted to face forward while walking instead of continuing to leer at Derek Davis. She tripped over her own feet and stumbled. The basket she was carrying fell onto its side, but her messenger bag stayed securely in place. June quickly helped her and brought her back to her feet.

"Did he see that?" Farrah said.

"Yep."

CHAPTER EIGHT

FOR the first morning of appointments, June handled everything efficiently for Farrah. Farrah even got that lunch break she was promised. She was starting to feel the fatigue after four back-to-back hours of such physical work. The adrenaline kept her going, but it wouldn't last. She couldn't wait to sit down and replenish herself.

The main dining hall was decorated hardcore in the forest hunting lodge motif like the rest of the building. The expanse of the great hall was filled with people seated at long wooden tables and benches. There was a buffet, carving stations, and a dessert spread that looked to die for.

"Let's grab trays and plates. I'm starving! I don't know how after everything I ate at breakfast," Farrah said.

June got behind her in line and scanned the room to see if any of the executives from the earlier incident were there too.

"You know, if they were all wearing robes this would look a lot like wizarding school."

"Most of us wish it was," Derek said surprising them in line.

"Oh, hello. You'll have to excuse June. She needs practice speaking in a lower, less offensive volume."

"But notice she didn't say I need to say less offensive things. Wizards are not offensive, by the way."

As they continued down the line, Farrah was happy to see more food choices she could have than on the restaurant's menu. Small talk never relaxed Farrah. It filled a void though. Eventually, the trio engaged in more interesting details.

Derek said his morning included a sunrise yoga class in a solarium that overlooked the lake. Then he did one of the less physical sessions where people were paired up to do a drawing game - one person had a shape to describe but wasn't allowed to use the name of the shape while the partner had to draw it. It was supposed to help with overcoming bad communication skills and misunderstandings. Before lunch, he joined one of the hiking teams for a short outdoor session.

"Wow," Farrah said. "I guess I have no right to complain about being fatigued. How much more do you have to do today?"

"I'm going to try the rope ladder and save the rock climbing for tomorrow. I love that kind of stuff. Not to brag, but I have my own gear."

"Oh," June said. "You're one of those."

"One of what?" he said.

"You probably have a dating profile with photos of you doing all these rugged activities. How many are shirtless? Come on… tell us."

Derek laughed, but confessed that she nailed it as well as any mentalist.

"I am divorced and my dating profile does have those kinds of pictures, yes."

"Are there cock shots?"

"June!" Farrah backhanded her reasonably hard on the upper arm.

"What? It's a legitimate question! That's what some people do on those sites."

Derek turned eight shades of red and laughed some more. He denied that such tawdry selfies existed on his pages. Yet he didn't deny that they existed on his phone.

"No, no, no. It's okay. I like women who speak their minds." He made an attempt to regain his composure. "I'll let you in on a secret."

They all leaned forward in a huddle over the table.

"Most of these people are completely pretentious. The ones who do speak their minds tend to be… shall we say… abrasive? Yeah, abrasive works."

"So what does that make you?" June continued to be one hundred percent herself.

"Oh, I have to fake a lot at my job. Nowhere else, mind you. But in the trenches, you need to play tough and kiss some ass when necessary. Be great on a team, but take the fall alone if something goes bad."

Farrah finished the last bite on her plate and saw an opening presented. "Something bad? Do you mean like those protesters before? Is one individual going to take the fall for that debacle?"

"Good question. I don't know the answer though."

June's curiosity was also piqued. "Have you had to take the blame for something other people did at this company?"

Derek was silenced for the first time. He used the opportunity to finish a cup of cottage cheese with oats and raisins sprinkled on top.

"I was the lead on the team that was supposed to make a huge deal in China. We couldn't make it happen though. And after they invested millions of dollars into trying to make that happen, someone had to be held accountable."

"They didn't fire you?" June said.

"No, but they fired my boss and I basically have to serve penance. I haven't gotten a raise or been a team lead since. Honestly, except for the raise part, I'm relieved. I'm not working the grueling hours I was. I'm managing to get out and enjoy life. I wasn't able to do that before."

Farrah enjoyed getting to know Derek. She hadn't had a real conversation with a man in a long time. Her conversations with Jackson seemed to only revolve around their marital problems.

"How long ago did all that happen?" Farrah said.

"Three years ago."

"Did you keep in touch with your old boss?"

"Once in a while. I heard he went into non-profit work, but I don't know the specifics."

Farrah and June were invited to go along with Derek on his next team hike. It wasn't Farrah's normal type of thing to do, but that was precisely why she said yes. It was time for her to live a little too. She warned him that she'd slow them down, but he didn't seem too concerned. June, however, was interested in the hike for the actual hiking experience not for the flirting opportunities.

"See that woman over there?" Derek said, pointing to a woman in her late forties wearing jeans and a sweatshirt with the company logo on it. "That's Chloe Griffin, the head of Human

Resources. She's a Grade-A bitch. When they were coming down on me hard about my boss not sealing the deal, I had to spend a considerable amount of time in her office. And because of my normal reaction - I mean, who wouldn't be angry - she forced me to take a course in what they called Stress Management. But it was really about how you shouldn't yell at the HR department. Needless to say, I was not alone in that course. There are an abundance of Caressa Lamour employees that vent too aggressively, it would seem."

"I guess I can see why the company needed to have a retreat like this if people butt heads that often and that badly," Farrah said.

"It's normal in any company, especially one this size."

Derek could've continued to sound like a bitter jackass, but instead he steered the conversation towards Farrah. Although he was gossiping, he showed off some manners. He politely included June in the conversation even though it was clear Farrah was the one with his interest.

Farrah talked about her less than stellar and still burgeoning massage career. She caught herself talking too much about her old one and her old life. The words kept pouring out her mouth uncontrollably. He wasn't a psychologist, but he may as well have been, because she felt good unleashing all of it on him.

"If you guys don't mind," June said, "I'm going to head out. I'd like to get to know the layout so I have an idea about where we'll be setting up the portable chair and making sure the spaces are adequate."

"Oh, I better go with you," Farrah said.

"No. No. I got this. You have another half an hour for lunch and you need this break."

After June walked away, Farrah's concern was obvious from the look on her face.

"Is everything okay?" Derek said.

"I don't know. That was strange for her leave me like that." Farrah was instantly regretful of how her words could have been interpreted. "I mean, it's no big deal. But she's been a great asset to me on this trip. I don't know what I'd do without her."

"Listen, since you have some time left, you don't need to spend it in a noisy dining hall. Do you want to go for a walk?"

She had no idea why she said yes other than having no valid reason to decline. It was just a walk. A simple walk. Two relative strangers becoming friends over lunch and then a walk. Nothing salacious, she told herself. Plus, it was something she could handle easier than trying to keep up with a large group.

Autumn in the northeast had a distinct earthy smell that lingered on the air. There were breezes blowing through the tall oaks, maples and big tooth aspens. Decorative mums lined the walking path around the building but gave way to more naturally occurring plants en route towards the lake. Their steps crunched and snapped the fallen twigs and dead leaves against gravel.

"Thanks for this," she said.

"For what?"

"Suggesting the walk. The fresh air is wonderful. I'm always recommending things to my clients that I never do myself. I can't remember the last time I went out for a walk for no other reason than to enjoy it."

"Nature seems to agree with you. You're smiling. It looks good on you."

She shook her laugh in disbelief not only at the cliché but the thought of enjoying nature. That wasn't her scene. She was an indoors person. Being in a comfortable chair with the cat nearby and some crime drama on TV.

"Derek, you have no idea how funny that is. The amount of time I spend outdoors is going from the house to the car then the car to the massage studio. Nature and I have not had a romantic history."

She was aware that he kept looking at her face. She hadn't been seen like that in years. It was an observing style like another human being was studying her and learning. No one watched her that way except maybe June, but they spent so much together, it never felt like a crash course of her body and spirit.

She wanted to look at him too but felt awkward about it. She noticed what she could like his slight limp which she tried to diagnosis in her head. He kept clean-shaven, at least so far being the first day of his week away from his office. He didn't drink coffee which was sacrilegious in her eyes. He kept a healthy diet, had interesting hobbies, and was in fine shape looking easily ten years younger than he was.

They spent the rest of the time avoiding subjects like jobs, her marriage which she merely mentioned and moved on, and the murder investigation a month ago which she did omit entirely. She certainly didn't think it was the best ice breaker to talk about being a murder suspect, and if she mentioned that she helped solve the crime, it could come off as bragging and unbelievable. Anyway, that kind of drama was behind her. She didn't want to look back at the moment when her career was in jeopardy and her name was a trending hashtag.

When it was time to return to the real world of appointment books and team building exercises with apparently contemptuous people, Farrah physically felt heavy energy descend through her core. It was the sensation of disappointment. Logically, she did want to return to work. She was enjoying it after all and happy to be earning some money, but she also didn't want her conversation with Derek to end so soon.

CHAPTER NINE

AS Farrah walked in front of Derek on a narrow part of the path, her pants got caught on a thorn.

"Here, let me help you with that," he said and was about to kneel down to dislodge her from the bush.

"I'm fine! I got it." The tingles in her nerves told her that if she let him get that close to her legs, she'd be tempted to let him get that close to every other part of her body. She bent forward and plucked the branch from the fabric.

"These are my favorite scrubs," she said. "I'm glad they didn't get destroyed. Bad plant!" She playfully pointed a corrective finger at the shrubbery when something shiny caught her eye in the distance.

From where they were standing, they were about to break through to the part of the path that wasn't covered by trees. It was a plateau that overlooked Lake Ahchuwikee glistening under the sun. There were big rocks and signs of the drifted shale layer encroaching the region from the west. The ground dropped off to a landing area fifty feet down. This was where Shawnee Conference Center professionals took stressed out corporate employees rock climbing.

"Looks like someone might have dropped something over there. It could be important like a phone." Farrah pointed and lead the way towards it.

They sped up their pace and found the object that was dazzling in the sun. It was a silver carabiner clip used in rope ascension and repelling. They knelt down to look at it and Derek picked it up.

"Looks like it hasn't been here long. It's not covered by dirt," he said.

"Oh my god! Derek! Look!"

Below on the dirt landing, a man's body was sprawled in a contorted pose.

"I think that's Milton Byron!" he said.

"Do you know how we get down there from here?"

"Only by the ropes. I'm sure there's another way, but I don't know the grounds either."

Farrah immediately called June who answered the phone asking why she wasn't back yet.

"June, stop! Listen to me. I need you to go find someone from the lodge security staff or maybe a manager and the person who teaches these the rock climbing lessons. We found a body."

"Another one? What is with you and dead bodies?"

"June! Just get us some help!" Farrah continued to explain where they were located and gave instructions for June to post a sign that she wouldn't be making her appointments. Then she told June to bring the navy blue backpack which contained a first aid kit. This guy looked like he needed a whole lot more than first aid, but it was something to do. Meanwhile, Derek was on the phone with 9-1-1.

If Milton Byron needed CPR, it was going to be too late. It took five minutes for the first wave of onlookers to gather. June, Cynthia from the front desk, and Bob the maintenance worker were the first pack.

"Markos and the owners of the lodge will be here as soon as possible," Cynthia said. "I spotted Forrest on my way over here and told him to grab his climbing gear."

"Is there any other way to that spot?" Farrah said.

"By boat of course, but there are longer trails that would get there. You have to hike a pretty indirect route. The only direct path is straight down."

June handed Farrah the backpack. She unzipped it and pulled out the first aid kit. She looked up and saw Forrest Finch running towards them with two coiled up ropes and a couple harnesses. The introductions between Farrah and Forrest were efficiently brief.

"Have you used your first aid training?" she said.

"Scrapes and cuts. That's it," he said.

"No lifeless bodies then?" she said.

"No," he said with a scrunched up face.

Was it so out of the ordinary to ask about lifeless bodies? Apparently so. June knew exactly what that meant. Farrah should be the one to examine Milton first so that Forrest could be at the top of the plateau keeping her safe on the rope and acting as her anchor.

"I'm an experienced climber, Farrah. Shouldn't I go?" Derek said trying to act like a hero.

"And do you know what to do if you find a pulse on him? No? Okay then. Make yourself useful by making sure I have this rig on right." She didn't even take a beat to let Derek answer her question. In her mind, it was rhetorical. She was going down there. She would redeem herself after the way she mishandled the murder at Riverside Wellness Spa.

Forrest gave instructions to Farrah about how to get over the cliff with a firm stance and pivot over the side. Derek continued to interject his expertise, such as it was, but there were definitely too many alpha males barking orders.

"Would the two of you shut the hell up? I need you to keep me safe. You can whip them out and measure them later! Got it?"

June pretended all she was doing was giving Farrah a hug, but she whispered in her ear. "Damn, girl. That was awesome." She smiled and gave the harness a tug to make sure Farrah was secured - not that June had any idea about that gear.

Forrest finished up his quick tutorial about releasing the rope and belay orders that Farrah would have to shout up to him. He and Derek still thought they were the best people to descend, but Farrah knew she was the best person present to tend to the patient, if necessary. She snapped on a harness and was ready to go. They would have to work as a team if any of them wanted to rescue Milton.

Farrah leaned back at the edge with straight legs. As the old saying goes, the first step was a doozy. She shimmied baby steps for the first ten feet then sprung out and down like she was supposed to. She controlled the breaking of the rope with her right hand behind her back and held onto the other end of the line with her left. Looking back at June and then focusing on the edge right behind her heels, Farrah took the first step down to a rock that jutted out. The few seconds she was there making sure that it wouldn't give way felt like hours.

"Keep going. You got this," different people shouted. She had no idea who.

She looked up at June and saw her taking pictures. June gave her a thumbs up. She took another huge step and then the next and the next. She was doing it. She was descending over rocks for the first time.

The crowd flocked like lemmings right to the edge to watch her. June laid on her belly and gripped the dirt as if she was holding on to Farrah instead of the solid earth beneath her.

Farrah's pulse was easily over 180 beats per minute. She was hyperventilating and her palms were sweating inside the gloves Forrest gave her. The backpack felt like it tripled in weight.

Only a few more feet, she told herself. She shut out the voices from above yelling down to her. She tried to listen only for Forrest's orders. He directed her around an outcropping of rock. Ten more feet to go. Three more hops and she'd be on the ground.

One.

Breathe.

Two.

Breathe.

Three.

Solid ground.

Forrest kept yelling down. He reminded her how to unleash herself. She moved quickly, her hands shaking.

She ran to Milton and knelt down and tried to get a response from him.

"Milton? Milton? Can you hear me?"

She threw off the gloves and felt for a pulse at his neck. It was faint, but there.

"He's alive! Tell 9-1-1 to hurry the hell up!"

She turned back to him. "Milton. My name is Farrah and I'm here to help you."

Spinal cord injury was her main concern. She tried to examine him without moving him. There were faint signs of blood from the scrapes. The contorted position his body was in made Farrah think he'd broken all his bones. The most severe was a devastating compound fracture to his lower leg leaving the bottom of his pants soaked in blood. If not for the fabric, Farrah would have seen the bone protruding right out.

What good was a measly first aid kit? She was in over her head. She should have let Forrest come down. There was no way a couple of bandages and some tape would do Milton any good.

She took out the scissors and cut open the pants from the ankle hem to his knee. She may have spent many years working in a hospital, but she was a desk jockey and never had to get close to the gore.

"We're gonna need an Aircast," she shouted up to the crowd.

Farrah picked up Milton's hand. "Milton. Milton? Can you squeeze my hand? Can you do that for me?"

The thumping rotation of the helicopter blades beat across the sky. It took a moment before Farrah could spot where it was. She had no idea where they would be able to land. The plateau didn't have many trees, but there were a few. The parking lots were filled with cars. The only other choice would be the lake if there was some way for the chopper to land in the water, but not all of them could do that.

Police arrived on the scene with a crew of paramedics. They looked down the cliff and saw Farrah with Milton.

"Milton, please squeeze my hand." Still no response. He hadn't spoken. His eyes were closed.

Then her phone rang. The display said it was June, but it was one of the officers asking her for an update. She relayed that he was breathing and had a pulse, but it was weak as far as her untrained skills could ascertain.

"The medevac can't land."

CHAPTER TEN

FARRAH couldn't believe what she heard from the officer in charge on the clifftop above her. The helicopter couldn't land.

At least they could avoid a daunting search operation and focus on rescue only. The emergency medical technicians that arrived by ambulance stood by waiting for the chopper crew to make the rescue. The police officer, Sergeant Caldwell, took authority of the scene.

"We're going to need a cast and a spineboard at the very least. And I don't know how to use those," Farrah said to him over the phone.

"The medevac has two paramedics that have more experience in this sort of thing. They'll land the chopper nearby. The ambulance is going to pick them up and bring one of them here as soon as possible. One of our local EMTs will assist him."

"And then what? You'll have Forrest lower them down?"

"That's the new plan."

"Okay. I'll try to keep Milton comfortable, but he's unresponsive."

While they waited, a blanket was lowered down for Farrah to keep Milton warm. She checked his pulse every minute out of nervousness of not having anything else to do, but also to update the team at the top. Ten minutes later, two EMTs descended to her. By then, Milton's pulse was gone.

The two medics moved so quickly, Farrah thought it was kind of inhuman. She was in awe. She never spent time in the hospital's emergency room, but she had a feeling it was like this. They spent less than a minute to get him onto the spineboard.

The medic checked his pulse again and shouted that it was gone. They'd need to resuscitate. One medic did chest compressions while the other tended to his leg.

"We need the paddles."

The helicopter medic ripped open a bag with the portable defibrillator machine and got the charge going.

"Clear!"

The ground medic quickly released his hands and backed off the body. No pulse.

"Clear!"

Still nothing.

One more time… "Clear!"

Finally, a heartbeat returned. The helicopter was

overhead lowering a rig with additional board support. The EMT that remained on the chopper with the pilot lowered a powered hoist for their partner to be pulled up. Farrah kept watch over Milton and soon he was lifted up too and in the relative safety of the medevac with the two EMTs.

Now that the serious issue was over, Farrah needed to get back up to the landing with everyone else. Since Derek knew how to ascend, he rappelled down with Forrest's lead and helped Farrah. He threaded the ropes through her clips and instructed her on how to use ascender devices which would allow her to scale faster than if her first-time hands pulled her up on the rocks.

She looked up at the top and saw people peering down waiting to congratulate her on being heroic. Farrah took out her phone from the cargo pocket of her scrubs and dialed June.

"Hey, how many people are up there?"

"About twenty right around here at the edge, but there are people all over waiting to take your picture and be part of the spectacle."

"Tell Forrest nevermind. If there's a long way on foot back to the lodge, I'll take that path the ambulance couldn't take."

Farrah released the safety of her carabiners and stripped out of the ropes. She left on the harness, but took off the helmet and carried it since she'd have to give those back to Forrest anyway.

"You can go the hard way. Point me in the right direction of the trail and I'll go the long way."

"Nah, that's okay. Call them back and tell them I'll walk with you." Derek removed his helmet and looked around the area for other loose items to take back.

"Suit yourself." Farrah texted June the update. The dangling ropes looked like eels slinking back into a cave as Forrest pulled them up without climbers.

The shoreline of the lake was rocky and caused Farrah to stumble a couple of times. They followed the water for half a mile and spotted natural steps that formed from roots of a giant tree.

"That was interesting," he said.

"Looks like your people will have more to talk about than animal rights radicals."

"I wonder what will happen now," he thought out loud more than asking her. "I'm sure we'll stay here and continue. They won't cancel the retreat."

"But I bet they cancel the rock climbing sessions."

"Maybe. I don't know. I bet anything Brad Dubray and Mary Woodson follow Milton to the hospital. Do you know this area? Any idea where they'd take him?"

"I have no idea, sorry."

They made it to the man-made part of the trail clear of growth. Farrah wasn't sure if they were still on the lodge's property of if they crossed into the county park trails. It felt far.

"I better message my boss to see if she's still stuck in Florida and to tell her all this. I missed a lot of appointments and honestly, I don't know if I want to stand and work right now. I need a shower and want to rest."

"Your first climb under stressful circumstances? I can understand the need for a nap."

It was chilly and Farrah was still sweating from the climb, the stress, and the walking. Needing a shower was an understatement. She was dirty and her scrubs needed to be changed. The adrenaline rush began to recede and made her nauseated.

"Farrah, wait," he grabbed the shoulder strap of her backpack and made her stop. "Let me carry this. I should've taken this from you sooner."

"You're a gentleman, but it's not that bad. It felt a lot worse coming down those rocks."

He insisted and helped her slide the pack off. She got a better idea of his physique through the tight jersey knit shirt he wore. He was dressed like the outdoor extreme sports were his profession rather than wheeling and dealing cosmetics contracts.

His shoes probably cost more than Farrah made in a month.

"Aren't you cold?" she said.

His smile was killer. "Not while I'm moving and being physical. It's pretty pleasant actually. Is there room in this for the harnesses?"

He unzipped the bag and poke around through her things. There was plenty of room since she had unpacked half the contents with her setup in the massage suite. They fit the harnesses in and resumed the long walk.

"It was smart thinking for you to pack a first aid kit. Who would've thought to bring one?"

"It's not like I used it much. I didn't save his life or anything. I cut his pants open and the professionals arrived."

"You took charge. You descended a cliff for the first time. You kept everyone else informed. Give yourself some credit, Farrah Wethers."

"Thank you for that. I went through a difficult emergency situation before and I was useless. I was frozen in panic. I thought I was going to lose my job. I was pretty sure I was responsible for it and so did everyone else until we realized what happened." It was hard for her to keep up at Derek's pace despite his limp.

"Sounds mysterious. Are you going to tell me?"

"Not a chance," she laughed. "You can Google me later.

Right now, I'm enjoying someone talking to me without prying me for scandalous gossip. I don't socialize much. Except for June. We're together most of the time."

"Oh, um… are you two…?"

"No, we're not a couple. I'm married… to a man, I mean. I thought I mentioned that."

"Maybe you did and I was trying to forget."

Farrah knew her heartbeat was fast from walking, but there had to be a considerable contribution by Derek too. She didn't know what was going on. Could he possibly be flirting with her? When was the last time anyone did that? Besides some drunks in a bar, she couldn't think of a single time it happened in the last fifteen years. Men who flirted with her weren't genuinely interested in her; they were trying to sell her something. But this guy, Derek, he seemed into her. Her cheeks blushed and she had no idea how to wrestle the feelings that flipped around inside her hormonal middle-aged brain.

"The lodge should be just over this way," he said. They took the right at the fork in the trail.

"What do you suppose Milton was doing there by himself?"

"I hadn't given that any thought. Why?"

"Doesn't it seem odd that your boss fell down a cliff? Was he drunk in the wee hours of the morning? Did he trip? How long had he been lying there?"

"Wow, you ask a lot of questions. I don't know. I guess I thought it was just an accident. Sure, Milton drinks, but I can't say I've ever seen him stumbling drunk."

While they walked, Derek tried to steer the conversation back to Farrah. He asked her about her interests outside of work. She tried to do the same, but her concentration was off its game.

"Was Milton a good boss? Was he liked?"

"Back to Milton again. Okay. I can see I'm not interesting enough," he joked and flashed that smile again. "I'm kidding. Milton was pretty likable for a CEO. I mean, how much do you really know someone at that level, right? He was always professional. He's been working hard for the last eighteen months on drilling into us this team building and waste cutting stuff."

"But I guess it's safe to say all the animal rights people hate him, right?"

"Oh, sure they hate anyone. That's the way radicals are. If you aren't one of them, they hate you."

Farrah prodded for more information on why exactly the BARN organization hated Milton and Caressa Lamour. Derek said it didn't make any sense. Their skincare and cosmetics are labeled cruelty-free based on the definition of it as spelled out by the US FDA. They've had a third-party audit done every year to keep their status.

"I've heard that BARN is willing to get violent. They claim to be these peaceful, loving types, all lives are sacred and whatnot, but they make threats against living breathing humans and corporations that employ a lot of people. Do you know if they've ever followed through and hurt someone?"

Derek didn't know any more than she did. BARN was the type of organization that, on the surface, seemed to have logical missions and objectives; but groups always splintered into factions. BARN's official mission didn't include targeting celebrities and fashion designers with fur coats to throw red paint on them; but the people who did that in the past were dues-paying members of BARN.

They reached the end of the trail and walked across the grounds to the main building. Derek emptied Farrah's backpack and took the helmets and harnesses back to Forrest. Farrah headed directly to her room for a shower. She texted June with her status update. She sent a long text message to Samantha explaining the situation. June was inside the massage room at the desk rescheduling the clients.

Farrah enjoyed the hottest water she could tolerate cascading over her skin. She washed off the dirt and grime with a lemon verbena soap. The towels were luxuriously plush like being encased in a cloud of cotton. She wrapped herself up and laid back on the bed. She closed her eyes and Derek popped into her thoughts. Muscular, lean, not too tall, flirtatious Derek Davis.

Without any logical stream of consciousness in her head, Jackson popped into her mind. She didn't know whether to text him or not. Would even care about what a disaster her trip was or what she just accomplished?

CHAPTER ELEVEN

FARRAH hesitantly hung up the soft towel and got dressed in a clean set of casual clothes. Since June was canceling her appointments for her, she didn't need her scrubs. A pair of khakis and a decent looking shirt would do. She pulled her wet hair back into an elastic and twisted it around into a bun.

She walked over to the massage room to take over for June who already had half the clients rescheduled. June kept meticulous records of her phone calls. She even posted updates to the new social feeds she made for Farrah. They included photos of Farrah's descent over the cliff, tending to Milton Byron, and helping the paramedics.

"I can't believe you posted these," Farrah said. "What if Milton or the resort sues me for this?"

"Oh, stop. They can't sue you for this. You were a hero. Someone got hurt on their property which, by the way, probably should have had signs and a railing, and you put yourself in danger to help him. That's great PR. Trust me."

June decided that they needed food to help Farrah recover. The shower did wonders, but she was still in a state of disbelief. They looked online at the menus for the dining hall and the restaurant and June left with an order for soups, sandwiches, cappuccinos, and iced tea. If it was all going to be charged to their room and paid for by Caressa Lamour, they weren't going to skimp out. They agreed to meet back at their own suite.

Farrah rolled her shoulders back and steadied herself. She tapped through her phone's contact and made the unfortunate call to Samantha to fill her in with as much detail as possible. She heard a click which broke up some of Sam's words. She looked down at the screen quickly and saw a text came through. Sam was still chatting away and oblivious, so Farrah had to wait for her to take a breath and interrupt her.

"I'm sorry to cut you off, Sam, but I have to get back to these messages and firm up the schedule."

"Normally, I'd say we could give them all a discount on an upcoming appointment, but chances are you'll never see these people again. Plus, they aren't paying out of pocket for any of it. The company is and the company can afford our rates. No discounts this time."

They ended their call after Farrah promised to keep Sam updated constantly. The text message was from June. It seemed alarming since she wrote it in all capital letters.

JUNE CHO: MILTON IS DEAD!!!

Wait… What? Farrah couldn't believe what she just read. She messaged back for more information. While June was in the dining hall, she heard people talking about the bizarre incident of their CEO being found at the bottom of a cliff. June, being the friendly and curious person she is, butted her way into the conversation.

It turned out that Milton's personal assistant, Mary Woodson, did go to the hospital with Brad Dubray. Milton would have been heading into surgery, but he didn't survive the transport. He died in the helicopter when they couldn't keep his heart going.

Everyone in the company received messages from the head of human resources, Chloe Griffin, to gather in the dining hall at four o'clock. Her message briefly conveyed that Milton died and the scheduled workshops were canceled for the rest of the day. More information would be given to everyone when they assembled.

June returned with the food. Farrah told her about her call

to Samantha first then wanted all the details June had.

"Everyone was talking obviously. It's so bizarre. There are already fantastical rumors flying like that he was so upset over the animal rights group that he leapt to his death. That's how wild the stories get."

"Jeez, could that even be remotely true? Would someone as together and successful as Milton Byron jump off a cliff?"

"I doubt it. I'm not saying a powerful, successful person couldn't be depressed or suicidal, but not that method. That seems far-fetched compared to something like hanging, pills, or a gunshot, ya know?"

"I know what you mean. I think jumpers have a different type of thinking. I don't know much about the subject, but I bet each type of attempt could be categorized or profiled psychologically."

"What about opportunity? Maybe Milton was waiting to be away from his family."

"I have no idea. I can't accept a driven CEO giving up under stress. That's the type of position where you only get to that point because you can handle the stress. Something isn't sitting right with me on that theory," Farrah said.

June gave more details about her prying. She had asked the pack of employees about Milton's home life. That's how she discovered that he's been married to his third wife for seven years and has five children from the different marriages. He had only been with Caressa Lamour for two years and was brought in by the board who ousted the last CEO. He was the type of leader that came in, cleaned house, stayed for a couple years to show higher profits, and then would bounce to the next opportunity.

"So, he was probably on his way out already if he'd been with them for two years?" Farrah said.

"I think that's a safe assumption. There were layoffs last year with his belt-tightening practices. People are scared again that more are going to be cut because of this controversy with BARN. Maybe not layoffs though. Whether it's one person or several, they only have a few hours left to defend themselves against the accusation that they test on animals and someone's head will roll for it."

"True. BARN gave them twenty-four hours until they release the videos they claim to have."

Farrah's email inbox and social media suddenly blew up. The photos and posts June made for her got the attention of national news media. Reporters were writing to her for interviews. Blog sites made her viral. A lot of people were claiming her escapade to save Milton Byron wasn't real because her accounts were so new and had few followers.

"They don't think I'm a real person? How can that be? I'm right there in the photos!"

"It's life on the internet, my dear. Just wait, it gets worse."

"Worse? I don't want worse, June! Take it down! Take it all down!"

"Farrah, sweetie, it's too late. Once your posts have been shared and reshared and screen captured, it's too late."

"What are they going to do?"

"They'll try to find out if you're a real person and if those photos are fakes or not. They'll dig and dig. We used your real name and business information, but they'll get your private address and stuff in a matter of seconds."

"June! Why didn't you warn me about this? Why did you insist on setting up these accounts?"

"I'm so sorry, sweetie. I was only trying to help you market your practice. I'm really sorry."

Farrah covered her face with her hands and lost control. June had seen her cry plenty of times, but not because of something she caused.

Farrah's phone rang. It was Jackson.

"What the hell is going on, Farrah? Why are people calling the house, calling me, camping out with cameras on our front lawn! I got a call from the neighbors that our block has been taken over by reporters and god knows who else! I checked the house messages and it's filled with news stations asking for your side of the story and a bunch of wackos. Side of what story?" Jackson's tirade went on to explain that several of the messages on the voicemail and emailed to him were threats. Vile threats. Disgusting anonymous statements describing where, when, and how they wanted to rape his wife.

Farrah was sickened by what she was hearing. Her husband was distraught. She felt like he was blaming her for garbage that people on the internet were saying and doing. She refused to tell him that June was the one who posted the news about her attempt to save Milton Byron.

"This is how people treat a hero, June? This? They harass my family? They threaten to rape me? They say they know where I live, where I work, and are camped out on my lawn? June, what the hell am I going to do?"

"This is how women are treated, sweetie. I'm so sorry you're finding out first hand." June put her arms around her and kissed the side of her head. "You're not going to go home, that's for sure. We'll call the police. I'll screen capture any threats that come through social media. You can save any that come through your regular email. We'll make sure the conference center has some security in place and we'll just stay put here."

"But why would they threaten me for trying to save someone?"

"Because they have no lives of their own. Because as soon as a woman is praised for something, they'll do anything to knock her down. Some of them could be lunatics that are taking this animal rights stuff too far or at least pretending to be part of BARN when they're really cowards that hide behind a screen and have nothing better in their lives than feeling like they have control over the internet."

"Delete the pages, June. Just delete them."

"I can, but it's honestly too late. They know where you are."

The feeling of being violated crept through Farrah like a parasite. She trembled at the idea of people around her house, looking in her windows, going through her trash. What if they broke in? What if they hurt her pets? What if they hacked her bank accounts? She had to turn off her cell phone when it wouldn't stop ringing. This trip started out bad and dove into nightmare territory fast.

CHAPTER TWELVE

FARRAH spent the time she needed to process her feelings while staying locked up and hidden in the suite. June took control and contacted the front desk and demanded that their highest person in charge of security and the manager of the conference center come to their room immediately.

June didn't delete the accounts, but she did click through the complicated settings and turned all the feeds to private so that from that point forward, anyone wanting to follow Farrah's news feeds would need to be approved. She screen captured what she could and saved the images to new folders on the laptop. She set up saved searches to make it easier to keep track of every time Farrah, the Shawnee Conference Center and Resort, Milton Byron, Caressa Lamour, and Riverside Wellness Spa were mentioned. It was a lot of work to curate, but she knew she was responsible. Even though half of the people on top of that cliff were taking their own photos and videos and posting them, June was the one that created Farrah's online presence.

The knock at the door startled Farrah. She was on a loveseat gripping a throw pillow into her, curled up like a scared child, and crying on and off at the fear of people tracking her down.

"It's okay. It's Markos from the lodge's security office," June said after looking through the peephole.

"The manager can't be here right now, but I'll fill him in on everything. I gave him the heads up that there were threats against someone staying here, so he could begin to inform the staff." Markos entered the suite but declined to sit.

Markos Demisovski was intimidating. He stood like he had military in his background, but that could've meant he was a cook not infantry. His uniform was the darkest blue possible. He was dressed like a casual version of a SWAT officer. Farrah felt a little bit more protected having him there.

June explained all the details and showed him the online activity. The posts varied from people cheering Farrah for being a hero to derailing the conversation to animal rights activism to threats against Farrah, Milton Byron, the retreat center, and Caressa Lamour's facilities. Some were peaceful political stances of consumers calling for boycotts against Caressa Lamour until they stop animal testing. But then the worst things imaginable, things Farrah couldn't even imagine, were posted. Her naiveté regarding life on the internet made her feel stupid.

"Your friend here is right, Ms. Wethers. This is exactly how people behave online. If a woman runs for office, this is what she goes through. If an actress portrays a strong powerful female superhero, this is what she goes through. It happens through every industry from tech and video games to social activism."

"You can't be serious! This can't be real."

"I'm sorry, ma'am."

Farrah was in no position to mentally process everything that he was saying. She knew there were good people and bad people in the world. She knew evil was out there, but she could not understand that some of them would be offended by her simple act of kindness. It made no sense. The world no longer made sense.

"Have you checked in with your family?" Markos said.

"My husband. He's at work for another hour or so. But not my daughter. She's in college. Do you think I need to warn her? Do you think she's in danger?"

"Unfortunately, yes. You need to contact her and her school immediately. There's always a chance that someone will send a bomb threat, no matter how fake, to her school. It needs to be taken seriously. As does any threat against this facility, your office, your home, and even your husband's office. Sergeant Caldwell, who was here earlier during the rescue, is coming back and we're drafting a joint plan and statement to go out. Oh and you may want to contact your banks and credit cards too. Just in case."

He never sat down until he needed to say one thing to her. Then he crouched down on a knee in front of her curled up body.

"I promise you, Ms. Wethers, I'll do everything I can to keep you safe."

Markos left June and Farrah alone in their suite. Moments later, another knock was at the door. Farrah was busy calling her daughter to explain the unbelievable situation she was in while trying to sound like she was composed, confident, and not afraid.

Derek entered the living room area and sat on the loveseat right next to Farrah who was still clinging to the throw pillow and talking on her phone.

"Honey, please do what I'm asking. I'm not saying you need to skip classes or anything. Just keep your guard up. Stay off social media for a few days until this blows over. And if you ever feel like someone around you is being suspicious or if you get sent any terrible messages like this, please go to the campus police immediately and call me." She hung up and tried to inhale as best as she could. It wasn't easy. Her chest hurt. Her eyes were swollen from crying. Her face burned from the tears.

"Hey," Derek said. He put a hand on her knee. "I wanted to see how you were doing after you had some time to decompress, but it looks like I walked in on something serious. Do you want to tell me what's going on?"

June stood several feet away out of Derek's eyeline and watched him put his hand on Farrah as if they were old friends. She retrieved a cold bottle of water from the refrigerator and knelt down next to Farrah.

"Here, sweetie. Drink some water. So, Derek, what brings you by here right now, right at this particular moment?"

"I wanted to see if you two were going to the four o'clock assembly. I'd walk over with you, but it looks like something bigger is happening here."

"Yeah, something big is happening here," June said.

"June, it's okay. He's a friend."

They filled him in on the crisis and he was shocked. Like June, he had heard of this sort of backfire and cyber harassment before, but had never been in the direct sights of it.

"Markos said that he'll be making a statement at the meeting to explain to everyone here about the best practices for security like using the key cards and not letting anyone in the door behind you if they aren't showing their badge," June said.

"That sounds like a good approach. Are you coming? I'll walk you guys down. I won't leave you alone," he said.

"Farrah, what do you think? Should we go and find out the plan or wait here for people to get back to us?"

They didn't have much time. Farrah wanted to stay in the suite and hide. Something else compelled her to stand up. She tossed the pillow back on to the loveseat and took a swig of the water June gave her.

"Let me wash up and we can go over together," she finally said.

All the employees from Caressa Lamour and all the staff from the retreat center were gathered in the dining hall. Among those left standing, Derek, June, and Farrah tried to be inconspicuous along a wall. Farrah felt his hand rubbing her back up and down.

"You'll be okay," he said in her ear while he stood quite close so their bodies grazed each other.

His hand felt good. Better than good. It felt wonderful and warm. It was the kind of touch she missed and hadn't felt in a long time.

Chloe Griffin stood on the stage at the end of the long room. She said hello into the microphone and it squelched feedback. When she was able to begin, she welcomed everyone politely then got down to business. She announced the death of CEO Milton Byron, which wasn't news to anyone at that point. Then she gave more courteous commentary on what a capable and stoic leader Milton was during the short time he was with Caressa Lamour. Finally, she hinted that there were safety concerns and introduced Markos Demisovski who reviewed the protocols at the retreat center and strongly emphasized suggestions about online activity.

People formed a line at a microphone on the floor to ask questions. For the moment, everything was being directed towards BARN as the culprit. One brave or possibly stupid Caressa Lamour employee, Sagari Palla, introduced herself at the microphone and asked if one of the protesters could have come back and pushed Milton over the cliff.

Everyone murmured and gasped. They had the same thought, but no one else would have had the balls to say it into a microphone in front of a thousand people.

Farrah turned her head to Derek who still had his hand on her back. "Who the hell is Sagari Palla?"

"She's in sales. Kind of mediocre in performance. Keeps to herself. I don't know her that well at all."

Markos waved his arms like he was patting the air so try and calm down the crowd. He was well-rehearsed, it seemed, in using his voice and body language to come across with authority. He assured all of them that the local and state police were going to have a presence at the retreat center for the duration of their corporate event. The state police has one mounted officer on horseback as well as two canine units.

Activities, except for the rock climbing, would stay on schedule. The rock climbing area would be reassessed for safety including recommendations for a guard rail and installing lighting. No one was expected to hide indoors. They would remain perfectly safe as long as they followed the guidelines. He said all staff at the center had been given a refresher in what was expected of them as well.

"If Caressa Lamour isn't canceling the retreat, I guess we better stay and work," Farrah said as they walked back to the room.

"If you want to cancel, I'm sure your boss would understand. I have no doubt that Brad Dubray would understand," Derek said.

"Brad? The ass-kisser you pointed out? That's who's in charge now?" June said.

"He's next in command. The board will still have to make formal nominations and vote, of course, but if it's not Dubray, it'll be someone from the outside."

"Thanks for walking us, Derek, but I think June and I would like to be alone in our room the rest of the night."

He asked for her number so that he could check in on her later. Before he left, he said he would gladly escort them to breakfast the next morning.

"I'm surprised he didn't offer to sleep on the couch to keep an eye on you all night," June said once she and Farrah were inside the room.

"And would that have been so bad?"

"You tell me. Would it be so bad that you'd hide that little fact from Jackson?"

"I don't know. I really don't."

CHAPTER THIRTEEN

TUESDAY

ON Tuesday morning, Farrah and June planned to get back to a working schedule of massage appointments. Just like he promised, Derek texted Farrah before bed and again in the morning. He offered to escort them from their room to the dining hall for breakfast. Farrah didn't want to seem to so dependent on a man who wasn't her husband in front of June. She compromised and told Derek to meet them there.

"What are your plans today, Derek?" Farrah said.

"Yes, Derek, do you plan on being Farrah's bodyguard all day or do you have things to do?" June said.

Farrah shot June a look of daggers. Having someone around that made her feel even a little bit safer shouldn't have been discouraged. June unleashed this Pandora's Box. The least she could do was accept any offer of help possible for Farrah's sake.

"Uh... I honestly don't mind if you want me to tag along with you anywhere, but I'm not here to cramp your style."

"Don't mind her. She didn't sleep and hasn't had coffee both of which are vital to her."

He sipped his orange juice then tried to smile at June in an apologetic way. She may have felt guilty about the social media harassment, but Farrah was her best friend, not his. If she needed looking after, June expected to be the one to do it. That's why she was there working as her assistant instead of taking an actual vacation.

"As for my schedule today," he said, "I've got a team building activity on the ropes course right after breakfast. Then a break until lunch. And then... I'm supposed to have an appointment with you at three."

Farrah choked on a bite of crumbly coffee cake. She tried sipping her coffee to wash it down. Classy, she thought. Her face turned red and her eyes watered. She choked a couple more times before being able to speak. She had forgotten he said he had an appointment with her.

"I'm okay. I'm okay. Whew... yeah so, I guess I'll be seeing you then. June, what's our morning like?"

"We're supposed to move the chair to the alcove across from the solarium so that the people coming out of the partnered yoga class can get fifteen minutes each."

"Oh that sounds really nice. They have a small seating area there and tons of plants. It's looked so serene and peaceful. Not like the real world," Farrah said.

"Sweetie, we do have to face the real world eventually, but it doesn't have to be today. Anything we need, we can get right here," June said.

"Plus, I'm sure the lodge would be willing to bring in anything you need because of your special circumstances," Derek said.

Farrah was beginning to relate to celebrities who couldn't walk out of a door without being mobbed by paparazzi, stalkers, and gossip bloggers.

Derek introduced a new approach to her problems. He explained that he knew a bit about damage control from all his experience in the cosmetics and pharmaceutical industries. He said that if they wanted to alleviate the problem, they had to get out in front of it.

"Do you mean I should make some kind of statement?" Farrah said.

"Normally, I'd say a lawyer should do that for you. But I'm thinking I could talk to Brad and the people from our marketing department, and legal of course, to see if Caressa Lamour could make a statement thanking you for your bravery. But not just you, the entire rescue team. Even though Milton died, people risked their own safety to help him. I think it'd be good for Caressa Lamour and good for you."

"But even confirming that Farrah did the right thing won't stop the internet trolls. And don't forget," June said, "nothing is going to stop that video evidence getting posted by BARN today."

"Looks like all of us are having a PR problem," Farrah said.

"Farrah, I promise, I know this is bleak and scary right now, but by next week, the trolls will move on to a new target," he said.

"That doesn't make me feel much better. They shouldn't be allowed to go around threatening people like this. Bomb threats? Death threats? Rape threats? This is not okay!" Farrah said with as much gusto as she could without raising her voice.

Derek offered to cancel his appointment with her in order to give her an hour off. Farrah believed it was more about the obvious growing interest in her that he had. She insisted she was a professional and could get through her appointments just fine. Of course, that wasn't entirely true. She was a nervous wreck, but people were relying on her.

The countdown was ticking away. The BARN organization gave Caressa Lamour until noon to confess that they had violated the public trust and the regulations of the FDA. The deadline was four hours away.

Farrah and June retrieved the massage chair and supplies from the room then headed over to the quiet area by the solarium. It was almost time for the eight o'clock yoga session.

"Maybe I should've brought the table to assist people in stretching and cooling down," Farrah said.

"They're spending an hour helping each other stretch. I think the chair is fine," June said.

"Pssst," a voice called from behind a raised potted plant arrangement. "Pssst!"

June looked at Farrah who was busy setting up. She continued to look around for the source of the noise. A young woman's head poked out from the plants and she waved June over to her.

"Can I help you?" June said.

"Hi. Can you tell me if Brad Dubray is in there right now?" the young woman said.

"I have no idea. Who are you and why are you hiding?"

"It's a long story. But I need to talk to Brad right away."

"Are you allowed to be here? Are you an employee?"

Farrah noticed the odd behavior and approached June and the stranger. "June, what's going on? Who are you?"

She stood up and mostly came out from her hiding place, but she stayed close to it as if at any moment, she'd have to take a dive into the dirt.

"My name is Whitney. Whitney Gallagher. And I used to intern for Brad Dubray and we were very close. I have information that I need to give him."

"If you're so close, why don't you just email him like a normal person instead of skulking in the bushes?" June said.

"You make a good point. But it's because I'm sure his email is getting flooded, what with Mr. Byron dying and all that."

"I'm sorry," Farrah interjected, "I still don't know what you're doing here. Only authorized people with badges and ID are allowed in this building right now."

"No, but look." Whitney held up an authentic Caressa Lamour badge which she pulled from the pocket of her hooded sweatshirt.

"You said you used to intern for Brad," June said. "That badge isn't good anymore unless you're still an employee."

"Okay, well, I know the badge's magnetic strip wouldn't work in the Caressa Lamour buildings, but I showed it to someone who was walking in the side door here and they let me right in after them."

Farrah was furious and little bit scared. The Shawnee Conference Center and Resort and the police assured everyone that access to the building and the property would be strictly controlled. Not needing to swipe the corporate cards was a loophole they missed completely.

"I'm sorry, Miss, but I'm reporting you immediately. There are strict protocols in place for a reason," Farrah said and began to walk away determined to find a responsible staff member.

"Please! Don't!" Whitney said.

"Farrah, wait. Let's hear what she has to say." June's eyes intimidated the twenty-something into a submissive posture. Whitney slunk over to a chair and slithered into it. Farrah returned and stood with June towering over the girl.

"I'm with BARN... But it's not what you think!"

"Go on," Farrah said.

"I saw online the things that have been happening - the threats, I mean. I didn't have anything to do with that. I swear!" Whitney gripped the vinyl arms of the chair and leaned forward like a scared jack-in-the-box.

"Just get to the point. What information do you have?" June said.

CHAPTER FOURTEEN

JUNE and Farrah hadn't grasped the practice of Good Cop, Bad Cop. The fear, frustration, and anger had both of them wanting to be Bad Cop. Farrah had Derek's number and fought the temptation to text him and beg for him to come help. She had June; this Whitney person looked like she only weighed 105 so if she was physically threatening, they could probably take her. Unless she was wily and fast, of course.

Whitney loosened her grip on the chair and flitted her eyes back and forth from June to Farrah.

"I'm the one responsible for all this," she said. Farrah was impressed by Whitney's fortitude to look her straight in the eye when she confessed. But confessed to what exactly, she didn't know.

"How so?" Farrah exchanged looks with June and resumed their stare down of Whitney.

"When I was interning at Caressa Lamour, one of my tasks was to assist Brad and the regulatory director on audits. I had to go with them to one of the factories and record certain parts of the inspection. It was Brad's idea. He originally came from marketing and wanted to make some feel-good clips for the website to show how ethical the company was. Plus, he wanted proof for the external auditors who have been known to write up fake violations and extort a payoff."

"But I'm guessing you came across something not-so ethical after all?" Farrah said.

"I didn't even notice it at first. I was reviewing the clips and making sure they were what the PR department wanted in terms of content and then I compressed the files to send them to the ad agency."

"Hold on. Back up. I'm still dumbfounded that the auditors who check for ethical practices are secretly blackmailers. Why isn't that the story coming out on the internet?" June said.

"As far as I know that's true, but I wouldn't know how to prove it. It would launch a federal investigation here and no doubt another investigation in France where the corporation headquarters are."

It wasn't taking them too long to get the explosive information from the corporate mole, but they only had a few minutes before the yoga class let out and Farrah would be expected to work. She couldn't possibly cancel another morning's worth of appointments and still charge the company for her time. Farrah certainly aimed to be more ethical than the people who hired her.

"Okay, so there's corruption in the audits. But you said you found something that really did violate the regulatory standards. So it wouldn't be extortion if they were written up. Only if the auditors were given money to pretend they didn't see anything," June said.

"Now, Whitney, are you going to tell us what it was that you saw?" Farrah said.

"It's a lab," she gulped when she spoke. "I only saw it for a fraction of a second on the video. The clarity isn't great. It was something in the background. A door swung open and I swear you can see cages with something inside."

This was explosive indeed. If this video was what BARN was ready to publish, every news agency and animal welfare organization would jump all over it. Not to mention the public consumer base. If all those people bought Caressa Lamour skincare products believing the little bunny logo on the label meant it wasn't tested on animals, their trust would also be explicitly violated.

"Let me explain," Whitney said. "The truth is that no cosmetics products are truly, one hundred percent cruelty free. They get to say that if they base their quality control and testing on data that has already been substantiated for years. The thing is, that data all comes from other sources and those sources have to test on either live animals or cells acquired from formerly live animals. Even when they say they test on cultures only, those cells came from somewhere. But as it turns out, it's cheaper for this company to run its own testing lab than to rely on the outsourced reports. The animals and staff cost less than third party experts."

"I'm vegetarian and I didn't even realize this," Farrah said.

"Most people don't. It's an illusion. Like magicians. People want to believe it so they do. They want to shop and believe they are making a better choice."

"And they do it just to try and alter themselves to conform to beauty standards," June said.

"Exactly." Whitney appeared relieved rather than defeated.

"If you're part of BARN and gave them the evidence already, why are you here trying to warn your former boss?" Farrah said.

"Because I love him."

Farrah's hand came up to her face and covered her eyes. This stupid, stupid, stupid young woman. She fell in love with her boss who was now the head of a multi-national corporation which would be exposed for the unethical treatment of animals and a number of broken laws. And she wanted to warn him that the evidence was real.

"I know what you must think. Why didn't I just tell him right away? Why haven't I texted him? We were having an affair and when my internship was over, I thought he was really in love with me too. I thought we'd be together. But he stopped answering my calls and messages. Then one day, he said he'd call the police if I kept stalking him. That's what he called it! Stalking! After he led me to believe we'd get married someday!"

Poor Whitney was broken down. She sobbed and hid her shame in her hands. Farrah retrieved tissues from her tote bag of supplies and gave some to the distraught naive activist.

"It's not stalking when you have a weekly date to have dinner and sex with me, is it? That's not stalking!"

"Girl, you should want revenge not protect his ass." June knew had seen this a million times in television dramas and women's literature.

"I have to agree with my friend here. If he treated you so badly, why would you even want to warn him?"

Whitney snorted up her runny mucus and continued with her revelations.

"I did get mad. I got furious, in fact. That's when I asked Chloe in HR if I could return to the building because I forgot a hard drive in the desk that I needed for a school paper. She was hesitant, but she trusted me. I mean, come on, I don't exactly look like I'm capable of corporate espionage. So she cleared me with the security office and activated my badge for one more day. I went back, got the thumb drive, and left through a side door without going passed security and without turning my badge in."

"No one from security or HR noticed and asked you to return it?" Farrah said.

"No. They can activate and deactivate them without having the physical badge in their possession. So even though I have this," she held up her badge again, "I'm sure it's been deactivated already."

"Did you join BARN because you saw that lab or were you part of BARN all along hoping to find something to take down the corporation - that is, before you fell in love with the second-in-command?" Farrah said.

"I swear, I didn't join them until after Brad broke things off with me. I made a mistake! I didn't realize how radical they were. I didn't know they'd threaten anyone physically or dox anyone. I really didn't. I'm so sorry!"

The yoga class began to exit the solarium in silence. The Zen seemed to have done them a lot of good. They were smiling or had dopey expressions like they were sleepwalking. Brad Dubray was not among them. He was busy making the transition to CEO and most likely abandoned the rest of the retreat.

"There's only three hours until BARN posts it now. When they do, it's not just the video. They'll dox every single person they know is affiliated with Caressa Lamour," Whitney said.

"They got a head start, Whitney," Farrah said. Her eyebrows furrowed and her scowl sent Whitney back to cowering in the chair. The employees started to take notice of the disruption to their newly found peace. "They already began an attack on me because I tried to help save the former CEO's life! Now my house is practically under siege. I can't go home. I've been told to close bank accounts before they get hacked. My daughter is away at college hoping to avoid threats there. BARN started early, Whitney. They didn't wait until noon today to terrorize more people!"

The girl looked terrified. She would have to prepare herself to face Farrah, June, Brad, her fellow activists, the US government, and teams of lawyers.

"Farrah, you need to get started with those appointments

before they get suspicious," June said. She tugged at Farrah's arm to get her to move away from Whitney. "I'll take care of this. You have a simple release form all set up. They just have to use the stylus to sign it. You can handle it, right?"

Farrah nodded. Before she took on the first client, she told Whitney and June that no one should have to go through what she and her family were going through. No one should have to worry about their accounts being hacked, threats to their homes or their jobs, or threats against their children. She wanted them to figure out how to stop the extremists from revealing all that data especially considering how many Caressa Lamour employees were innocent and had no idea they were breaking the law.

She hoped that the tension coursing through her tight muscles wouldn't be noticed by the clients. She faked a smile and greeted the ten people who were gathered around. They were instructed to stay as quiet as possible while she played music on the portable docking station. If they could continue their meditations until their turn at the chair, no one would realize that Whitney was sobbing and frightened next to the planter box. Farrah hoped that in two and a half hours, when all the morning clients were done, that she'd be able to gather Derek, June, and Whitney to come up with a plan to stop the footage from leaking thirty minutes later.

CHAPTER FIFTEEN

FARRAH had to keep the back massage appointments a few minutes short of their standard fifteen in order to clean the chair between clients. She also needed to constantly check her phone which was buzzing endlessly from social media notifications, messages from Sam and her daughter, and at one point a voicemail from her husband. The clients didn't seem to notice. At least they had the decency not to complain that they were shorted any time.

She looked at the schedule on the tablet to see who was up next. The name rang a bell, but she wasn't sure why at first. Seeing people dressed in yoga outfits or outdoors gear was different than how they dressed for meals and she hadn't gotten a good look at faces.

"Sagari Palla?" Farrah said as she scanned the final six clients waiting patiently. There were only two Indian women waiting. Farrah assumed Sagari must be one of them and she was correct. A tall, thin, dark skinned woman that looked like she stepped off the fashion runway stood and approached her.

"That's me." Sagari didn't have much of a smile. Farrah noticed there was a hint of sadness that the woman was trying to mask.

Farrah bustled around to clean the chair and put on a fresh cover for the donut-shaped face rest. She finally remembered Sagari as the woman who spoke up during the meeting.

"And how was your yoga class? Were you able to relax at all?"

"It was fine. I'm still tense. My muscles haven't quite let it all go yet," she said. "I wish they scheduled some kickboxing here."

"Punching your stress away is one good alternative," Farrah said hoping her smile would help comfort the woman. "Let's see what I can do for you."

Sagari signed the tablet's e-signature space for the release form. In Farrah's standard chair routine, she focused on the back, neck, and arms. She discovered Sagari's stress pent up in her shoulders and her hands. She was probably the type of person to grip a steering wheel hard or clench her fists in frustration if she felt she couldn't express herself; not to mention all the typing and texting expected of people in the corporate world.

"Let me know if this pressure is uncomfortable."

Sagari lifted her head from the cradle and turned it sideways to speak to Farrah quietly.

"It's wonderful, but I don't know if the best massage in the world could crack through my stress. I'm so worried about losing my job. This scandal could force another major layoff. My baby is only six-months old. I need this job." She started to cry, but quickly wiped away the one tear that was allowed to fall and pulled herself together.

"Oh, I'm so sorry. Maybe it won't come to that." The lilt in Farrah's speech didn't exude any confidence. She knew there was no way to stop the controversy from getting worse since it had already begun the day before.

"I warned my boss about that animal testing weeks ago. He ignored me so I went to the CEO. They both made me feel like I was some unhinged, irrational woman that doesn't know anything about this business."

Farrah saw that Sagari's hands were clenching the padded rest. She took action calmly and confidently. At least this part of her job, she knew well. She moved her hands up to Sagari's head and gently guided her to rest it back into the face cradle. Soothing strokes along her neck followed. She walked around to the front of the chair and kept her hands on Sagari's arms until she worked her way down to her hands. She had to work around a fair amount of gold rings and a bracelet, doing the best she could. In a matter of seconds, Sagari's breathing changed and her weight shifted while she began to relax again.

When Farrah finished up all the chair massage clients, she cleaned up the seating area leaving no trace of herself or the appointments. She begrudgingly played back the voicemail from Jackson.

"It's me. I'm taking Gordon to Frank's. We'll stay there for the rest of week. I'll check on Miles every day, but I don't want to be here. The reporters are too much. I'm leaving my phone on silent too."

No endearing "I love you" or "I miss you." He was all business. And unfortunately, that business was all unpleasant.

Farrah returned the equipment and supplies to the massage room to keep it securely locked up without having to store it in her suite taking up space. She received a text from June requesting to meet in the dining hall.

She found June with half her lunch already devoured. June had her laptop open and was engrossed in following the minute-by-minute activity of BARN and some hacktivists.

"Fill me in. How bad has it gotten?" Farrah said.

"As bad as you can imagine."

"Jackson left again."

"What do you mean? Left for good?"

"No, I think just for the rest of the week. He took the dog

to your ex's house. I swear, I wonder why he hasn't officially moved in with Frank."

"It's not easy for him either, Farrah. Plus, he wants you leave and move in with me."

"I know." Farrah was hungry. Emotionally, she wanted to eat an entire dairy-free pizza with a bucket of chips. Instead she got herself soup and a sandwich from the buffet.

"Where's Derek?" June said.

"He said he'd meet us here. I have to ask him something, so I wish he'd hurry up."

"Any word from your daughter?"

"She messaged. She swears she's fine. She promised to always have at least one friend around her at all times. Luckily, the school took me seriously. They were honest though and said there was nothing they could really do unless a threat came to them directly. Hopefully they'll step up patrols though."

Derek entered the spacious room. His hair was wet and his clothes were fresh. He must've showered after the ropes course. Farrah got lost in a tempting thought of him in the shower with hot water running down him and steam rising, among other things.

The pleasantries exchanged were benign except for his dashing smile. Derek was still leaning more towards openly flirting with Farrah than she would in return, in front of June and other eyes anyway.

"The hammer is coming down. Hard." He sat upright and tense. His phone firmly gripped in one hand, the other flat on the table. "Brad, Chloe from HR, and Milton's former assistant Mary left the conference center last night. We've already gotten emails announcing Brad as the interim CEO. Hopefully Mary isn't out of a job because he's not required to take Milton's assistant as his own. But it looks like a lot of people will be canned."

"Are they doing it as punishment for the animal testing or as punishment for the leak?" June said.

"Good question. Doesn't really matter. There's a lot of blame going around. They'll sue anyone who violated their non-disclosure agreement, that's for sure. And if somehow, someone who wasn't authorized got that footage, they'll be arrested for trespassing at the very least. But knowing corporate legal teams, they'll be able to drum up a variety of charges."

Farrah almost forgot what she wanted to ask him. She caught a light whiff of rosemary and ylang-ylang coming off her clothes and it jogged her memory.

"Who does that woman Sagari work for? The woman that caused such a commotion at the meeting asking if Milton was killed by a protester?"

"Oh, her. She's a little out there, if you know what I mean. I think her looks got her this job because she doesn't have a real aptitude for it." Farrah and June weren't quite sure what he meant and the look they gave each other telepathically relayed their mutual concern.

"What do you mean? Was she bad at her job?" Farrah said.

"She's a hard worker, don't get me wrong. But she's aggressive. Fierce. For example, in meetings, she acts like she needs to command attention instead of just talking in a normal tone."

"Uh huh," June said with clear intent.

"So a woman in a board room is aggressive and it's a negative thing, but if it were a man, it's be totally normal, right?" Farrah said it and she nailed it. She also had the sense that Derek's perception was a bald faced lie. She had met Sagari. The woman was timid and scared. Not aggressive or abrasive.

"No. No. I don't know. Maybe. I guess," he floundered. "She's trying too hard. She also has a tendency to poke her nose into projects that aren't hers. It's pretty undermining and conniving. I'm not saying that it's because she's a woman."

Farrah gave June that mindreading look again. Yes, it absolutely was because Sagari was a woman. As Farrah got to know Derek, he increasingly became less of a dreamy fantasy and more of a disappointment. She still couldn't help the hormones inside her that wanted to rip off his clothes though. And due to her job, she actually will have his clothes off him after lunch for his full body massage treatment.

"But to answer your earlier question, she worked under Brad like me. He was our vice-president. But now with him as acting CEO, that means there will be a nice opportunity for someone to get promoted. Someone besides me, of course. I think I'm still on the blacklist because of that China deal. Why do you ask?"

After hearing some of the ways Derek talked about people and his glaring ego, Farrah was no longer sure she could trust him. She decided to play it cool and fill in June later.

"No reason." Farrah wouldn't divulge that Sagari mentioned her boss was stressing her out.

Farrah's phone buzzed. She normally left it on vibrate in her pocket during work sessions. She pulled it out, saw it was Jackson calling again, and excused herself from the table.

"I tried to go to the bank on my lunch hour and my card wouldn't work. I went inside to find out what was wrong and they said our account was on a security lockdown. Even with my identification proving I'm really me, they wouldn't let me take out any money, Farrah!"

Farrah had called her banks to warn that there might be hacking problems, but she thought that meant they would add some additional tracking or fraud protection.

"Jack, I'm sorry. I called the banks to ask them to watch for unusual activity. I didn't know they'd freeze the accounts."

"I called them when I got back to my office and kept escalating up their staff until I could speak to a person who could actually help. That took about six transfers and whole lot of wasting my time!"

Somehow this would be all her fault. She got up from the table and finished the call out of earshot.

"Would it help if I called them back?" she said.

"No. They said there's a block on everything. Eventually I was connected to someone in their fraud department who confirmed that it was basically some kind of hack attempt. People kept trying to guess our passwords and it triggered a freeze. This isn't good."

"I know it's not good, but what am I supposed to do about hackers?"

Jackson knew there was nothing either of them could do except wait for the heat to pass. Hopefully, like June, Derek, and Markos said, once the trolls found a new target, they'd forget Farrah Wethers was ever in the news. She prayed that would be soon. She hung up and returned to the table and filled them in on the latest attack against her and her family. It was going to take another week for the banks to issue new credit and debit cards and migrate all their funds to brand new accounts.

"It's not like we have a lot of money. We're struggling middle class people. We pay our taxes. We keep our noses clean. We donate to charity. Why the hell would people do this to us?"

"I told you," June said. "It's because you were praised for trying to saving Milton who is now under the microscope for a huge scandal. That makes you guilty by association or something."

"She's right," Derek said.

"I want my life back," Farrah said. She felt the most defeated she ever had in her life. And to make it worse, her opponents - the people who were winning - were nameless, faceless ghosts in cyberspace.

CHAPTER SIXTEEN

FARRAH fought with her own stamina limitations to enjoy the lunch break and feel some sense of renewed energy. Every time she thought about this situation of threats, harassment, and hacking, her body wanted to collapse. It was a physical struggle as much as an emotional one. She didn't even know what doxing was until this crisis. She and Jackson were in it together as far as she was concerned. Without his support, the funds being cut off was one more thing to beat her down.

Her home was supposed to be a safe place, a haven. Home is where you go to rest, feel loved, and welcome friends. It should never be the place where you feel in danger or violated. Jackson was gone. Their daughter was hours away. They had no access to money. And she found herself neck deep in a maniacal battle between activists and a cosmetics corporation. She wanted peace. She wanted her family or something that felt like family. She wanted the normalcy that once bored her to tears.

"I'm sorry, sweetie," June said. "For what it's worth, Markos came and escorted Whitney quietly to an office here at the lodge."

"Whitney? Whitney who?" Derek said.

"She said she was Brad's intern," June said.

"Oh, her. We're all pretty sure they were hooking up. Why is she here?"

"Yes, it seems they were secretly dating," Farrah said. She explained that Whitney admitted to be romantically involved with their boss. She left off the part about Whitney giving the footage of the lab to BARN. "She confessed that she joined BARN and was one of the protesters yesterday and how she sneaked back into the building. But she seemed more scared than anything. She certainly wasn't threatening when we talked to her."

June confirmed that Whitney was a blubbering, snotty mess.

Derek leaned sideways on the wooden bench to close the already small distance between him and Farrah. "She joined up with those lunatics? Wow! Do you think she's the one responsible for this nightmare?"

"Well, we can't be sure. We only know that she used to work for your company and now she's involved in the animal rights group." Farrah lifted the shoulder closest to Derek back and away from him. She wanted to keep the details of what Whitney said between herself and June.

Derek's hand covered the side of his neck and he rested the weight of his head supported by his elbow on the table. "Isn't that something? I bet it's all a hoax. I bet there is no evidence of animal testing and she started these rumors to get back at Brad for not continuing their stupid affair."

When they finished eating, Farrah said she and June needed to go over their records and the schedule before the afternoon appointments. There was no reason for Derek not to believe them. Farrah truthfully needed to talk to June alone away from the eyes and ears of Caressa Lamour employees.

"You do know you have to work on that man, right?" June reminded her.

"Yes. I know. I'll do whatever I can to be professional and simply pretend it's not Derek. It's just another body. I've seen hundreds of them. It's not going to affect me."

"You don't sound convinced."

"I'm not. But I'll be fine once I start working. Meanwhile, I need to know if anything more came out of Whitney. Then I'll tell you about Sagari."

June didn't have much to add about the broken-hearted former intern.

"I think they'll be putting the fear of God in her right about now. Markos is intimidating enough, but he doesn't have any kind of arrest powers as a security consultant. But he called that police sergeant to come back and talk to her."

"Seems like she made some stupid choices because she fell in love with the wrong man. We've all been there, I guess."

"That doesn't excuse her. She'll be held accountable for her actions if she's the one who gave that video to BARN. They'll get her on something. Corporate conspiracy or whatever the legal jargon is."

Farrah plopped down on the loveseat. She felt herself sink into the plush cushions. The maid service had fixed all the pillows so neatly, but she grabbed one like before to hug as a security blanket.

"Hold onto your hat. Whitney might not have been the leak after all. Sagari started spilling her guts during her appointment. It happens all the time. If people aren't asleep, I become their therapist the same way a hair dresser or bartender does."

"What did she say?"

"That she knew about the animal testing and that she's afraid she's going to lose her job."

June shoved Farrah's feet aside and sat next to her. "Did she say she saw the animal lab or the video?"

"Now that you mention it, no. She only said she knew about it."

They debated the likelihood of each person they knew to be involved and realized that they had created their own suspect list of people who could have leaked the video.

June noticed the time and opened her laptop. The twenty-four hours was up.

"Here it is."

She clicked through the source post since the video had gone viral in a matter of seconds and was embedded on multiple websites. BARN's site showed the clip exactly as Whitney described it. Brad Dubray was on camera bragging about the good manufacturing practices, or GMP, they have in place. In the background a person in a lab coat could be seen swiping a badge through a reader and walking through a door. As the door was opened, there were blurry things in the background. It was hard to decipher.

The website also had still images from the video enlarged with circles and arrows pointing to the blurs they claimed were cages of animals.

The war was on. Caressa Lamour's website was under a DDOS attack, a distributed denial of service attack, making it impossible to view anything on it that the user didn't have cached. BARN was able to corral and activate hackers from all over the world to bombard the Caressa Lamour servers.

"Do me a favor and pop over to the things you set up for me? Are they hacked too?" Farrah said.

"You have a ton of hate mail and shitty comments, but it looks like they haven't been actively after you since early this morning. They're after a lot of people at Caressa Lamour now."

"What else can you figure out?"

June found the hashtags that cultivated the news. One of them stood out, #TDCL. June scoured through the lines of comments and figured out it meant "take down Caressa Lamour."

"Honestly, Farrah, it's frightening how easy this was for them. There wasn't any security check in place when the conference started. One of the protesters walked in the front door and swiped one of the registration booklets off the table. All the employees who were here for the team building retreat were listed. That gave them a massive start. They had a list of a thousand names to search. Sites like ProKinect, Google and Radaris and all the social media networks lead them to people's personal information. Telephone numbers, home and work addresses, where their kids go to school. Everything. Most people aren't careful with that stuff. They post a photo of their kid playing a sport and if their profile lists their state, it wouldn't take much effort to deduce the name of the school. It's wicked, but it's easy."

"What do they do with all that data? What good does it do them?"

"Right now, these hacktivists and BARN are holding every Caressa Lamour contact responsible for deceiving the public and for abusing the animals. They've posted to a thing called pastebin where the data gets updated by whoever wants to add to it. They honestly believe there's nothing wrong with posting that information since it was public anyway. They see themselves only as curators not as violators of anyone's privacy."

"But after the data becomes so easy to find, anyone can start the process of identity theft, sending hoax threats or real ones, or actually taking it to the real world and physically assaulting someone if they wanted. My god, June. This is nefarious. It doesn't even have to be malicious viruses set off in networks."

"I'm sure that's being attempted. They'll break into people's accounts and post porn. That's one of their favorite things to do. They'll post extremely racist or sexist comments too," June continued. "Oh, and get this: they'll even make fake phone calls to the police claiming someone was seen with a bomb or a gun or is being held against their will and send SWAT teams to people's home addresses. SWATting has gotten so bad with celebrities that they had to define laws explicitly about it."

"Yeah I remember seeing that on the news when it happened to Ashton Kutcher," Farrah said.

June kept revealing more obscenely awful things being posted. She checked out a few of the feeds of Caressa Lamour employees and saw some were hacked and some weren't. The ones who weren't hacked yet posted about their fears of the situation and had repeating posts claiming they were completely unaware their employer was doing anything unethical.

"June, what if Milton didn't slip and fall down that cliff? What if Sagari was right and an activist came onto the grounds, targeted him, lured him, whatever - and pushed him?"

"It's a possibility, sweetie. If they were secretly here before the protest to swipe a registration book, then someone easily could've approached Milton Byron directly before the post was published online. It's not like he blends in. His pictures are on the Caressa Lamour site, the cover of the registration book, and he's been in magazine interviews. He stood out from the crowd here when they were all dressed in casual clothes and he was in a suit."

"I think our list of corporate spies is now a murder suspect pool," Farrah said.

CHAPTER SEVENTEEN

FARRAH and June returned to the massage room where June resumed working at the desk in the common area. Farrah put the finishing touches on the room where she worked on clients. She turned on the battery operated candles that she brought with her and set up the docking station for her music. She peered over June's shoulder to check the schedule one final time.

"What's the ninety-minute block? I was keeping my appointments to an hour."

"That was a special request. It was supposed to be for Milton Byron. But now that he's dead, I didn't know what you wanted to do with that time."

"Why don't you try to get a hold of Mary and see if she has someone to fill the spot? Maybe even herself. I'm sure after the last two days, she could use it."

"Or what about Brad Dubray? Maybe he's back at the conference too."

"It doesn't matter to me. If you can't find Mary's room, try that woman from human resources. Chloe something?"

"Griffin, I think."

Micah Maddox pushed open the door which June had propped open so it felt more welcoming and people wouldn't wonder if they were in the right place. They had him fill out the form and Farrah took him into the private room. She immediately thought he would make an adorable match for her daughter. He was shy but friendly; confident in his field but awkward about body issues. She tried to make him as comfortable as possible and left the room so he could get undressed and on the table.

"Oh my god, he's priceless," Farrah whispered to June.

"He's such a darling nerd," June said.

"He was nervous. Kept babbling. I should be able to get him to calm down and be quiet after a minute or two."

When Farrah returned to the dimly lit room, she sat on a stool at the head of the table. Fortunately, they remembered to pack one when loading all the linens into the van. Otherwise, she would have knelt for part of every session.

"Okay, Micah, I want you to start to relax. Take a deep breath and let it out." She had her hands on his head so that he would start to feel more grounded. "Is there any area where you feel like your tension is being held?"

"Well, I guess I get headaches a lot." His eyebrows furrowed as he thought about it. "And my shoulders are pretty tight. My grandmother always yells at me for not standing up straight."

"Grandmothers are good for that. Okay, let's see what we find. If anything hurts, you can just tell me."

As Farrah's fingertips massaged his scalp, his eyes started to close. He'd open them once in a while, taking in his surroundings. She could tell he was probably so used to being stressed that he didn't know what relaxed felt like.

"Besides the IT work and sitting at a computer all day, are there other activities you do?" She wanted to know as much as possible about his physical life. Whether he spent time at a gym or in front of the TV, his body would require different approaches on her part.

His eyes were open when he started to answer her, but then he felt her hands push into the knots of his shoulders and he was able to close them. "Um, I mostly sit in front of computers. Even at home. Or the TV. I get to walk a lot because I can walk to the train station from my apartment."

"Okay, and do you carry your heavy things in a backpack or messenger bag every day?"

"Yeah."

That explained some of the hunched posture. Months prior, Farrah read articles about children as young as elementary school students having issues with posture, sore muscles, and headaches from having to carry heavy books and laptops.

"You're the lady that tried to save Mr. Byron, right?"

Farrah was surprised to be asked. First of all, she thought everyone knew her by that point since her photos had been plastered all over the internet. Secondly, it wasn't common for clients to ask about her during their sessions. That was probably because the clients normally paid for their time, which was precious and expensive, so it was supposed to be all about them and their needs.

"Yeah that was me. I'm sorry I couldn't do more. I'm sorry for your loss. I heard he was a good CEO."

"Pfffft. Who told you that?" Micah's outburst and snarky smile startled her. "I guess people don't want to speak ill of the dead. But no, Milton Byron was not a good CEO."

"Oh, I'm so sorry. I didn't mean to upset you. Let's think about calmer things." She finished working on his legs and pulled the stool over to the far end to work on his feet. Head, feet, and hands - those were Farrah's specialties in getting people so relaxed they'd begin to drift off to sleep. Not this young man, though. He wanted to talk.

"You're not upsetting me. Not at all. I just think it's

hilarious. This guy comes in - he was an outsider - the board puts him there to be their puppet. Then he does two waves of layoffs in his first year. He cut benefits. Everyone who wasn't kissing his ass, walked on eggshells around him. Some of the cuts he made actually made sense and weren't punishing the rank and file. Like, for example, he wouldn't renew the country club memberships for the higher brass. They were pissed, but that made the minions like me happy - the ones that kept their jobs, that is."

Farrah was used to the candor of her clients. Like she said plenty of times, they unloaded frustrations and drama on her all the time. The closed room, dark atmosphere, and the sense that the time was to focus on them, were all things that gave clients a sense of personal security. She was told about affairs, struggles with raising kids, confessions by people who admitted sometimes they thought about running away and escaping their responsibilities. She heard a lot of sordid things. Of course, sometimes the stories were so good she told June, but never mentioned the people's identities.

"Well, I'm glad you got to keep your job. A big company like that seems like it would have a lot of opportunities for someone your age." She tried her best to stay positive and lighthearted, speaking of the silver linings and all the crappy clichés about doors closing so other doors could open. Having been through the layoff nightmare herself, she remembered what people had said to her. Luckily, this kid survived the cuts and got to keep his job.

"My team is packing up now. We have to get back to deal with the hackers. I didn't carpool with them so I said, screw it, I'm keeping this appointment for a massage and then I'll go back. We probably won't get any sleep for the next week."

"Good for you. How many IT people came to the conference?"

"Not many. We couldn't tell if it was a punishment or a bonus. I mean a week away from our desks sounds nice, but when you consider how long it takes to catch up when you get back, it's a pain in the ass. And it's not like this is a vacation. It's not work, but we're still here with coworkers to improve our communication and interpersonal skills or whatever. And in IT, we get pestered all day and night anyway. People never treat us like we can be off the clock."

It didn't look like Farrah was going to put Micah to sleep or even into a dopey trance. He was fired up. He seemed to be enjoying her work, but one hour was not going to be enough to help this boy unwind.

"Honestly, I hated Mr. Byron. I hated him and I hate everyone on that board. I sure as hell hate that weaselly Brad Dubray who is replacing him."

Farrah didn't respond to that confession. She could have said a variety of things like, "you're too young to be so bitter," or "you have skills so you can start looking for another job," or "being a CEO can't be easy." Instead, she redirected back to pitching ideas for him to implement into his life to help his posture and stress management. Somehow, she didn't think he would be the type to keep exercise bands at his desk in order use a ten-minute break to reverse the damage of computer work, but she went over her standard recommendations anyway.

When it was time for Micah to leave, Farrah hoped she would have five minutes to talk to June. That didn't happen, because sitting there waiting for his appointment was Derek Davis, the strange man that she couldn't figure out. Was he friend or foe? Was he a confident gentleman or an arrogant chauvinist? All she knew for sure was that he had a way of making her forget about her personal drama.

Derek Davis.

Farrah's professionalism would be put to the test working on him, that's for sure. It wasn't hard for her to look at his naked body as nothing more than a specimen that required therapies and treatments. The hard part was going to be not talking to him the same way as clients like Micah.

She didn't want Derek to open up about anything while on her table in a candlelit room with the soft sounds of babbling brooks and dulcimer tunes. What if he confessed something that made her feel awkward? What if he got too personal? What if he brought his flirtatious nature into her professional setting?

It was no place for coy banter or for him to put his hands on her for comfort like he did during the company's meeting or when he helped her up the hiking path. She certainly wanted his hands on her and she wanted him to say sweet things to her, but not there. It was wrong professionally, for one thing; and wrong because even though Jackson wasn't treating her like a wife, she was still married. She was seconds away from pretending to be sick to get out of it.

CHAPTER EIGHTEEN

FARRAH lead Derek into the room and ran through her rote explanation about what a client should expect one of her full body massages to be like.

"I used to get worked on by sports trainers all the time, but never anything in a peaceful setting like this," he said.

"I'm glad you can still call this place peaceful after the protests and losing your boss in such a tragic way."

"We have to move forward, right?"

As much as Farrah could appreciate living with momentum of moving forward and not looking back, there was something too snarky about the way he said it.

Farrah left the room for him to get on to table privately. She tapped lightly on the door to signal that she was about to come back in. She hated herself for the two seconds that she paused to ogle him. The sheet only covered his lower half. His chest muscles were sculpted better than most men ten years younger. He was a gorgeous specimen to study, anatomically speaking. As long as she continued to think of him that way, she didn't get nervous.

His lower half, even covered, didn't look as she expected. Farrah blinked and rubbed her eyes before approaching the table. The sheet unexpectedly was flat on one side.

"Do you mind if we talk while you work?" he said.

"Um, no. Some people do. Some people fall asleep. But it's about whatever makes you feel comfortable."

"Okay. I didn't know if you had specific expectations of your customers."

"Well, I expect people to be polite and respectful. But you're welcome to talk about what's stressing you out or if you have injuries that you need me to know about."

"Injuries? Well, I'm sure you've noticed by now." His hand pulled up on the sheet to reveal only one foot. A prosthetic lower leg leaned against the chair where he placed his clothes.

She didn't ask how or what happened. It was her professional responsibility to address his current state so she left it open that if he ever felt discomfort, if the pressure from her caused pain or wasn't deep enough, to let her know. She was surprised she hadn't realized it sooner. She noticed a limp, but since he was able to skillfully rock climb without much in terms of adaptive gear, Farrah was oblivious. She thought the special seat he descended with was something more advanced climbers would know how to use so beginners weren't offered it.

Derek stayed quiet for a couple minutes while Farrah worked. By the time she got to his left hand, she was the one who wanted to talk. Even in the darkness, she could feel the indentation where a wedding ring used to be.

"How long has it been?" She let her brashness blurt out.

"What?"

"Since you split up with your wife. It must not be that long."

"How did you know?"

"You haven't had your ring off very long. There's even a bit of a suntan line."

"I'm sorry, Farrah," he said lifting his head off the table to look her in the eye. "I didn't mean to keep it a secret or anything. I just wanted to try and not think about it for a while."

"So you're stressed about more than the China deal falling through and more than Milton dying? It's fine. You could've told me."

He put his head back down and she finished the session with nothing else noteworthy. Unlike her normally strict rules of confidentially, this land mine was something she would tell June since Derek had established himself as a friend before he was a client. Gossip wasn't professional, but it wasn't like they'd ever see him again after that conference.

She waited in the common room with June for Derek to get dressed. Her next client was already there even though she was scheduled for a 30 minute break to rest, hydrate, and stretch.

"Thanks for everything, Farrah. I'll text you later if that's all right," Derek said as he left. Even after she messed up his hair from working on his scalp, he still looked good.

"Sure." Her smile was more reserved than it had been interacting with him before. It was forced and polite. She felt different about him in some way. She tried to tell herself that his personal life was none of her business. He didn't exactly lie to her. He only failed to reveal a couple of things about himself and it's not like he was obligated to open up in the first place. She wrestled with why she felt guilty for having feelings about it at all. He wasn't a real friend. He helped her out during a difficult task, but soon, they would each be back in their own worlds. So why did she feel like he betrayed her?

"Farrah? Farrah?" June tried to get her attention.

"What? Oh, sorry."

"This is Chloe Griffin from Caressa Lamour."

"Hello," Farrah said.

"Hello. I'm not here for a massage. I came over to talk to you about something. Both of you."

Both Farrah and June were perplexed, but said they had a few minutes for her. June removed the wedge from the door and closed it for more privacy.

"Our legal counsel sent over additional documents for you to sign regarding your hired services here with us this week."

They took the papers from Chloe and scanned through them. They had the same reaction. Arched eyebrows from the surprise of being sternly handed non-disclosure agreements this late on their second day of working for Caressa Lamour.

"What is this about?" Farrah said.

"Oh nothing. Really. It's standard. All our contractors are required to sign NDAs, but yours slipped through the cracks somehow. Maybe it had to do with your employer being unable to attend. She would have been sent them originally."

"Samantha didn't say anything about signing legal documents when I talked to her. And I've talked to her several times already. I'm sorry, but I'm not comfortable with this," Farrah said.

"Me neither. You hired us to do a job and we're doing that plus more. This woman went above and beyond the call of freelance massage therapist and tried to save the life of your CEO." June put her copy down on the table and made no indication of picking up a pen to sign it.

"I promise you, this is perfectly standard operating procedure. All third party companies we do business with have to sign NDAs."

"I'm not signing anything regarding the arrangement Samantha Waterston and Riverside Wellness Spa made with you. Not until I send her a copy of this and get her approval," Farrah said. June agreed and added that their own lawyers should review anything too. Farrah hated to think about the last time she needed a lawyer which was when June helped her pay for a defense against murder charges.

"Of course. But you can't work on anyone else employed by this company until you do." Chloe's face had a plastered on pretentious smile. She turned away and exited.

"Shit. Now what do we do?" June said.

"I guess I call Sam. Again."

"I think this place has a communal business center. We can use their fax or a scanner, I bet."

"It's one monkey wrench after another with this assignment. I'm sorry I ever agreed to do this." Farrah took both copies of the document and tucked them into her portfolio.

"Should I cancel the rest of the afternoon appointments?"

"Not yet. Let's see if Sam can get back to me quickly. But make a sign for the door and say that we'll return at 3:30. If I'm still waiting, we'll have to turn the next person away and hope they don't hate us and do something like leave a bad online review. I've had enough of criticisms with this job - real and fake."

"This afternoon could make or break your spa's reputation. Not to sound like I'm blowing this paperwork out of proportion. And I did what you asked and filled Milton Byron's slot with Mary Woodson."

"And behind every powerful man is the woman who does all the work, right? You think Mary has more leverage than being just an assistant?"

"Maybe I watch too much TV, but yeah, that's what I think. When I spoke to her to see if the acting CEO would like the slot, she said he was too busy so I offered it to her and she accepted."

They left the suite and walked to the lobby to find out where the business center was. Cynthia, the brunette at the front desk who helped them check in on Sunday night, pointed them in the right direction.

"Did Mary say whether Brad was returning to the conference at all when she said he was too busy?" Farrah said.

"He's supposed to address the masses again tonight to give an update about the cyber-attack situation. I think these employees are having just as bad a time on this retreat as you are."

"Yeah, the IT guy said his team was heading back to the office already. Speaking of IT, what's the status of my profiles and pages?"

Farrah fed the document into a scanner connected to a reasonably sufficient computer. It was a bit outdated, she could tell by the speed, but it worked and got online.

"The heat seems to be off you. I think you're in the clear now if you want to call Jackson and tell him it should be fine for him and Gordon to return home."

"Thank you for handling all that crap the way you did."

"I was partially to blame for you coming under fire in the first place, sweetie. All I did was change all your passwords a couple of times since this started and made sure your settings were as private as possible for a business and swapped photos of you for stock photography."

Samantha called Farrah back immediately and said she'd review the agreement right away. With any luck, they wouldn't have to cancel any more appointments.

"Don't forget to delete those images from this computer. If it's so damn confidential, I don't want Caressa Lamour to accuse you of leaving corporate documents on a public machine," June said.

"Good thinking." Farrah made sure to Shift-Delete the file name and double check in the recycling bin on the desktop to make sure the document wasn't there.

They detoured to the dining hall to pick up a couple of cappuccinos and returned to the suite. A beautiful dark haired woman named Sandra showed up. She was another Caressa Lamour account manager. Farrah explained that they were expecting an urgent call and asked her if she wouldn't mind waiting a few minutes.

At 3:33, Samantha called back and said the document was fine for both of them to sign as long as they understood it. It was an NDA. It forbid them from discussing anything that they do, see, or hear during the week with anyone unless they receive authorization from the company. That meant Farrah couldn't talk to the press about her attempt to rescue Milton. She wouldn't even be legally allowed to tell Jackson anything about it. Plus, there was the obvious corporate gossip which Farrah already planned to keep to herself. That part she didn't mind. But if anyone asked her about Milton Byron's death, she'd have to keep her mouth shut.

"Do you think it's suspicious?" Farrah asked June out of earshot of the next client. "I mean, the part about not blabbing company secrets we might accidentally overhear, I get it, but come on. The rest of this? That we can't talk about Milton?"

"It sounds to me like they don't think his fall was an accident either and they'll do whatever they can to keep a lid on it."

"I guess we have to sign them or pack up and forgo the wages."

Both women were reluctant but signed the papers. Farrah got started with Sandra's appointment a bit later than expected, but at least she didn't cancel. While she was working, June called back Chloe Griffin and told her she could come pick up the contracts.

CHAPTER NINETEEN

MARY Woodson veered off the trend of Caressa Lamour employees talking during their massages. Farrah enjoyed the peace and quiet during it too. It was her last session of the day. Her own muscles were tight and tired. She felt the stiffness in her fingers and wanted to soak them in a bucket of ice.

"Thank you for offering the time slot to me," Mary said in the common room where June said at the desk monitoring the social media feeds.

"It's the least we could do," June said.

Farrah came out of the other room, wiping her hands off on a towel, then extending a handshake to Mary.

"We know you must be going through such a terrible time right now. I imagine Mr. Byron was a big part of your life," Farrah said.

"That he was. I was his assistant for nine years. He brought me over to Caressa Lamour when he was hired. A lot of top executives like to do that if they have good working relationships with someone. I had nothing keeping me where I was, so I packed up and took the job."

June expressed how impressed she was and said she couldn't think of any boss that she'd follow like that. She's had decent managers and bosses in her life, but none that she felt so connected to, she didn't want them to leave her.

Farrah leaned her hip against the table June used as a desk. "You must have seen every detail of his life after that many years."

Mary's face brightened a little thinking back over her years with Milton. She looked content and even proud as she spoke. But then, her eyes looked down and her brows crinkled up at the top of her nose.

"Things were different at Caressa Lamour though. It wasn't like our last employer. The reason the board brought him on was to fix everything that had gotten out of control. The divisions were doing whatever they wanted. People weren't working together. Milton's mission was to clean it all up and whip them back into shape to make the company efficient and strong again. Other artisanal manufacturers were the ones being covered by *Forbes*. Corporations like Caressa Lamour were old and outdated. They weren't progressive. Milton and I used to brainstorm about taking this company out of those dark ages and giving it new life."

Mary was clearly passionate about her role by Milton's side. It wasn't clear what her life without him was. Conversely, June had been working in county government almost her entire adult life. She was surrounded by female peers, mostly older than her, but it was usually men who got voted into office and made the critical decisions. Times had changed a little and there was one woman on the Board of Chosen Freeholders, but she didn't oversee the County Clerk's office where June worked.

Farrah, on the other hand, had been in small and large businesses. She saw St. Sebastian's grow from a local hospital to an acquisition of a healthcare network. Their small town physician atmosphere was erased to be a cog in the grand machine of patients as numbers and insurance company advantages. On paper, being her own independent contractor sounded idyllic, but she missed her benefits and paycheck.

"Where were you when Milton died or when you heard the news?" Farrah said. She was afraid she came across rude and shameless, but she wanted to know the answer.

Mary looked at her reflection in the glass of an ugly hotel picture. She used her hands to fix her hair then took out all the jewelry in her purse and put them back on. "Me? I was there with the rest of the crowd watching you try to save him."

"I mean a few hours before that. In the morning. Did you have scheduled activities when the protesters were here?"

"I have a busy schedule, but it's probably not like the rest of the staff. I had to be there to make sure Milton kept to his schedule."

"Which was?" Farrah said.

She put the backing on her last earring and examined her reflection again. "He had breakfast with Brad, Chloe the HR manager, and Micah the IT manager."

"And you were with them?" June said.

Mary told them that she was having breakfast with a couple of the assistants for the vice-presidents. Afterward, she returned to her own room to check her emails. She said after that, she started to head to her first activity in the Atlantic Conference Room, but that she got caught up in the lobby with everyone else watching the protesters. Milton was scheduled to be at an outdoor rolling log exercise that Mary wouldn't even attempt.

"But when we found Milton, he wasn't dressed for an outdoor activity," June said.

"No, he wasn't. He looked like he was in a business meeting," Farrah said.

"I guess he took a detour after his meeting before getting changed into sportswear." Mary's hypothesis was in line with everyone's.

They agreed that was a viable possibility, but he wouldn't have needed to go outside. The suites, the conference rooms, the business center, and the dining facilities were in the main building. The other buildings on the property included things like private cottages for parties of eight or more; a lot of storage sheds; and a couple of first aid cabins on far ends of the property for incidents too far from the lodge.

"Do you know for sure if Milton made it to his morning breakfast meeting?" Farrah said.

"Now that you mention it, no, I don't know for sure. They were in the smaller conference room for privacy and didn't need me to take minutes."

Without something like a coroner's report, Farrah thought about the span of time when Milton could've gone missing and ended up by the rock climbing area in his business attire. Mary mentioned the breakfast meeting was on Milton's calendar for eight and that his team building activity wasn't until nine. If he woke up, Farrah estimated, around six to get showered, dressed and maybe check his emails, but he never made it to breakfast, it meant he was outside before eight in the morning.

She didn't want Mary to feel like she was being interrogated and tried to keep their conversation friendly. Farrah truly did have intentions to be caring and kind to her clients. It wasn't often that she spoke to them for the sake of snooping. She offered Mary a bottle of water from their own stash which the woman declined.

"What will you do now?" Farrah said.

"For the time being, I'll work for Brad Dubray since he's the interim CEO. Whether they decide to keep him or bring in someone new, I'll be responsible for maintaining stability in the office. And if someone else does get the job, then I have no idea. I'll be there for a transition, but if there's nowhere else for me to go in this company, I have to start all over."

"Mary, can I be forward and ask you something?" June said.

"Sure. You can ask, but I don't know if I can answer. There's a lot of confidentiality in my job."

"Of course." June stood up from the desk and walked around the side of it to remove the barrier of furniture that was physically between them. "Did Milton know about the animal testing?"

Mary rolled her lips in the way someone would distribute their lipstick. Farrah noticed it and saw it as a sign that she intended to hold back words which she would have preferred letting out. Her fingers dropped to the desk and glided back and forth over the smooth wooden surface while she figured out what to say.

"Not when he took the job." They stayed silent waiting to see if she had more. "I'm sure, since you're in the medical profession, that you understand the kind of responsibilities and regulations that go into manufacturing products governed by the FDA. One of the challenges Milton faced was doing business in China where they naturally have their own set of regulations. To get any business there, a company has to show all the stages of testing that they require. That means it can be done by the raw materials suppliers as long as there is sufficient documentation, but that's new to this industry. China required animal testing by the final manufacturer until recently."

"Right," Farrah said. "We were surprised to learn that. I, for one, thought cruelty free labels meant there was no animal testing at all."

"The brand new product Rejuva-Complex skin cream was something that Caressa Lamour was working on before we came on board. It's revolutionary science. But it turned out, there was no raw material testing on animals. So in order not to lose millions of dollars on the product they had been working on for years, Milton didn't have any choice but to allow internal testing."

They didn't know what to say. Farrah had only been vegetarian for a few years and she was still learning the ways food, cosmetics, and even clothing companies were allowed to hide the ingredients that go into things. She would often have tirades to June about vague terms like "natural coloring" or "natural flavors." This revelation that "cruelty free" didn't mean squat was a brand new thing to get under her skin. While she tried to formulate thoughts on Mary's conversation, Farrah got momentarily lost wondering about all the massage creams and products she used for work.

She looked around for moment then her mind regained focus to continue the inquisition. "If that's true, if the testing was for this new Rejuva-Complex stuff, does that mean it would have stopped once the FDA approved it? Would the company be able to return to third party testing?"

"I can't really answer that with certainty. I've never been involved directly with the labs and the testing. As far as I know, once it was approved, those animals would be destroyed. And if any lawsuits or regulatory questions came down, they'd have to do it all again to confirm the original findings."

Farrah put both hands on the desk to stable herself. "I think I'm going to be sick."

"Thank you for the information," June said.

"Well none of this is secret," Mary made sure they understood she wasn't violating her own employee contract. "Documentation like this becomes public record once it's been filed. And they're looking to have Rejuva-Complex on the market in the next quarter. Look, I'm sorry, but I really should go. Brad will be giving an update to the troops in a couple hours and I have to see if he wants any slides prepared or needs me hold his hand."

"You don't sound very confident in Brad's leadership abilities," June said.

"He's no Milton Byron, I'll tell you that." After that odd sentiment, Mary Woodson left the massage suite leaving Farrah to clean up and June to make some end of the day posts online.

"What are you writing on there now?" Farrah said.

"I'm keeping everything saccharine and polite: 'Riverside Wellness Spa's massage team has enjoyed another successful day guiding Caressa Lamour's staff on their path to good health.' How's that sound?"

"It's fine, I guess."

Farrah picked up the jar of cream from the credenza and examined the label. There was the dancing bunny and the text saying the product wasn't made with animal testing. She felt betrayed. She knew she hadn't been one hundred percent cruelty free in the products she chose, but she made an effort. She probably had half or more with the bunny logo, but they were all misleading.

June looked up from the laptop. "One thing we do know for sure."

"And what's that?"

"Mary Woodson loved her boss and would never push him over a cliff."

"You know something though… she looked like she had a lot more to say. And even people who get along with their bosses have a bad day once in a while. I agree, she's at the bottom of the list, but I wouldn't rule anyone out at this point."

CHAPTER TWENTY

THE full body sessions were over and all Farrah wanted to do was eat and put on pajamas. She would not get her wish. She and June were about to return to their room when Chloe Griffin caught them exiting the massage suite.

"Ms. Wethers, we really need to talk."

"I don't understand. I signed what you wanted. I was allowed to work this afternoon if I did that. That's what you said."

"Why don't we go inside instead of continuing this conversation in the hallway?"

June turned around and swiped her key card in the lock. She flipped on a couple of lights and suggested they sit at the small circular table and chairs.

"Can I get you some water?" June said.

"No, thank you." Chloe put her black portfolio on the table and opened it up. She pulled out a document and a gold pen. "You see, right here," she used the pen to point to Samantha Waterston's signature. "Your employer signed this contract which states that Riverside Wellness Spa would provide three qualified massage therapists for five days. She hasn't been able to fulfill her end of the contract."

"There's a hurricane coming. She's stuck in Florida!"

"I don't know if you noticed," June interjected, "but the tropical storm was upgraded earlier today. It's not like Samantha can magically transport herself."

Chloe's smile exuded a brand of intelligent bitchiness mixed with conniving ambition. She laid the document on the folder and rolled the pen between her fingers.

"That's a shame. It's also not my problem. She has other staff members she could have sent."

"Yes, and the other CMT that was supposed to be here had her own emergency. Things happen. Life happens. Most of the practitioners are part-time. They can't leave their full-time jobs for a whole week." Farrah leaned into her words. She had to use her hands as brakes to keep from being too close to Chloe's smug face.

"What Farrah is trying to say is that Samantha and Christine had emergencies, unforeseeable circumstances. She still managed to do the best job possible under these challenging circumstances which, by the way, included trying to save the life of your CEO," June said in her own disguised way of calling Chloe and the company ungrateful bullies.

"I'm glad you brought that up," Chloe said.

Farrah knew talking to HR managers was trouble ninety-nine percent of the time.

"Caressa Lamour's legal counsel is launching a full investigation to see what role you played in the injuries of Milton Byron."

"You mean the role of rappelling off a rocky cliff to see if he was alive and then assisting the medics? That role?"

"Our team will be consulting with medical experts to see if anything you did contributed to his death." Chloe took out a wifi tablet from the pocket of the portfolio. She tapped a few times and spun it around for Farrah and June to see. It was a full video of Farrah's descent over the cliff and the time she spent with Milton on the ground. Farrah looked at the bar along the bottom of the movie. It was over twenty minutes long. Rarely did the camera shift to people at the top of the rocky edge.

"Did you shoot this?" June said.

"It's doesn't matter who did."

"Don't worry, Farrah, if this ever gets beyond mediation and in front of a judge, it'll be tossed out quicker than their insurance company can write a check."

"Anything else?"

"As a matter of fact, there is. Since your spa wasn't able to deliver the services promised, we won't be paying. That includes all your expenses too." Chloe put her things away and stood up. "I hear checkout is at ten. Have a good night."

Farrah gripped June thinking her best friend might assault the pompous woman leaving the suite. June rambled on and on at breakneck speed about how illegal it was for them not to pay for the services that were, in fact, provided. Farrah was already texting Samantha to see if she could talk. Unfortunately the reply she got was that she was without a hotel room and still stuck at the airport in Florida. Cities were without power and she was not able to help Farrah right that moment because she was conserving her cell phone's battery.

"What is with my life?" Farrah yelled. "Even when I try my hardest, nothing goes right!"

"Come on, sweetie. Let's leave your stuff until tomorrow. I'll go to the front desk and tell them to transfer all our charges to my credit card."

"June, you can't keep covering my ass."

"That's what friends do. If I wasn't able to, that would be different. I'd be honest with you. But this is fine. And unlike you, I will be back charging it all to Riverside. If you put it on your card, you could write it off on your taxes, but you'd still have to pay for it when the bill comes in."

Farrah wasn't able to walk away so easily from her equipment and supplies. She looked at it and tears welled up in her eyes. Everything in front of her was a physical symbol of her failing at getting a new career started: the massage table and chair; the linens and disposable covers; the oils; the reference books; the music; the laptop; and then of course, the creams with the bunny logo that she thought were made without animal testing. All of it sat there, mocking her.

"Leave it, girl. Let's go to the front desk and then get drunk over dinner."

June was right. Packing up the van after she spent hours working was not something her body needed her to do. She'd probably end up throwing the equipment too hard anyway and breaking it. Not to mention, her back would hate her.

They had no problems at the front desk switching the charges from the Caressa Lamour account to June's personal credit card. As they headed toward the restaurant, Farrah thought about two people and wondered if either cared about her situation.

"I think I'll text Derek and let him know that we're having our last supper and will be gone in the morning."

"I know he's been nice to you, sweetie, but I don't get a good vibe from him."

"Gee, you don't say."

"Was it that obvious?"

"The look on your face every time I mention him or whenever he's around is blatant. Look, I appreciate your concern and that you're looking out for me like you always have, but I want to enjoy something. Derek has been paying more attention to me in two days than Jackson has in a year."

"That's not exactly true. He was there during your legal troubles."

"Yes, but not romantically speaking."

"And you want to be romantically involved with a man you just met? A guy who is probably just playing you to get you naked?"

Farrah couldn't believe she spoke the words out loud. "Would that be so bad?" She was ashamed about having a fantasy.

"Why don't you divorce Jackson already? You'd be happier. It's been a long time coming."

"It's not that easy. Everyone makes it sound so simple to dump twenty years down the drain. He's taking care of all the finances. I can't leave even if I wanted to. Not with my failing business."

Farrah reached up to the bun on her head and pulled it apart. She tousled her sandy blonde locks with full-on "don't give a shit about beauty right now" attitude.

"If you don't want me to invite Derek to dinner, I won't. But I might want to see him for drinks later. Are you okay with that?"

"I'm not your keeper."

Farrah knew that June's feelings were hurt. They recently went through an emotional moment where June confessed her romantic love for Farrah. In return, Farrah panicked and tried to set June up with Jed the bar manager at their local watering hole, Happy's. It's not that June wasn't attracted to Jed's rugged country boy style nor that she wouldn't have loved some mind blowing sex. There were some heartstrings to break.

If Farrah desired time with this strange man over time with the person who has been there for her through everything, what did that say about her? Was she an awful person?

"I don't want you to feel abandoned. The only reason you're here is because I dragged you into this mess. I won't see him. There, decision made."

At that moment, when the hostess led them to a small table in the middle of the room, Derek looked at her from the bar. He didn't even ask if he was interrupting before coming over and pulling up a chair at the table which had been set for two.

"You don't mind if I play third wheel, do you? Our company meeting isn't until seven."

"We're having a pretty shitty day, Derek," June said.

"In that case, dinner and drinks are on me," he said.

"You don't have to..." Farrah began.

"You know what? This headache of mine is getting pretty bad. I'm gonna go lie down and call it a day," June said.

"No. Wait! Sit down," Farrah said.

June looked down at Derek. "And you were right, that HR woman is a Grade-A bitch. See ya later." She took her purse from the back of the chair and walked off.

"June!" Farrah stayed in her seat and let June walk away, but she felt terrible about it.

"Did I do something wrong?"

Farrah knew there was no way Derek could have been as successful as he was and be that incredibly stupid. Although, she did recall plenty of people getting promoted at her old job when they seemed to do the least amount of work and certainly weren't the smartest.

"She wasn't kidding when she said we had a bad day. Your company won't pay us for our time and won't cover our stay. They're considering suing me for Milton's death too. The only reason we're waiting until morning to leave is because I'm tired and June said she'll pay for the time we've spent here."

"That can't be right. They can't really do that to you. That would be another blow to their PR coupled with the current backlash they have."

His hand clasped around hers. She wished it meant something more. She wished all of his gestures meant something magical. She looked at their hands then pulled hers away. If they couldn't run away together, she had to stop that silly schoolgirl fantasizing.

"I'm sorry, I didn't mean…" he said.

"Don't. It's fine. I'm gonna go too. Maybe we can get help with all the equipment from their handyman and get the hell out of here tonight."

She looked into his eyes for as many seconds as she could stand it then she got up and left. When she got back to the suite, June was behind the closed door of her own bedroom. Farrah took her laptop into her room and pounded out a lengthy email to Samantha and her business partner Maggie Llewellyn demanding that they and their lawyer fix this ridiculous situation with their financial matters.

CHAPTER TWENTY-ONE

FARRAH looked at the clock in the corner of her computer screen. Her mind had a funnel cloud of thoughts. She wanted to check on June. She wanted to fill Jackson in on the continued turmoil of the job. She wanted to escape all of it and message Derek. Once her email to Samantha was sent, it felt like all those thoughts were biting her brain.

She slid the laptop off her legs, left her room, and walked through the living area. She knocked on June's door unsure whether she'd get a response.

"Come in."

Farrah sat on the edge of the bed next to June's feet. It was a natural instinct for her to put her hand on them and caress them.

"Are you mad at me?"

June's immediate lack of response spoke volumes enough, but she let out what was bothering her. Farrah didn't need her to because she knew, but the open conversation was healing.

"I just don't think he's good for you, sweetie."

"I know you don't. And he probably isn't. But you don't think Jackson is good for me anymore either. I love you, babe, but I can't have you hate every man that comes into my life."

"Sweetie, I don't. But I will keep looking out for you. Plus, I believe we have the kind of understanding that I can point out your bad decisions."

"Of course you can. I appreciate that. I know I don't always show it."

They came to an understanding and deeper appreciation for their pact of honesty. When they embraced each other, Farrah inhaled the light remainder of citrus fragrance in June's long silky black hair. She leaned back and held June's shoulder at arm length.

"June Cho, my dearest friend in the world, I love you and could sit in this big bed watching TV, but I still want to go get drunk and think of all the things I wish I could say to that bitch Chloe. You in?"

"You know, I think I'm good here. It's too dark to enjoy the view, but I know it's out there. Plus, that Roman bathtub is calling to me."

"Okay. I'm only a text away."

Farrah left her and was relieved to see a smile on June's face.

Back in her room, she opened the screen on her phone and tapped the texting app icon. The recent messages gave a clear account of her priorities. June. Samantha. Derek. Janice-Nova. Jackson was the fifth name down. She told herself that was perfectly normal. Couples weren't up in each other's faces constantly once they get passed that honeymoon phase. They've been through tragedies and stress on a regular basis.

When she opened the thread with her husband, she spent a few minutes scrolling back over the messages. She went back for weeks and couldn't find a single moment where he expressed love for her. She read his anger, panic, anxiety, and frustration along with benign messages about being at Frank's house. There was some concern for sure, but it was always about them as a unit, not specifically her. Not since the last catastrophe.

Bzzzt!

The ringer was still on vibrate. A text came through and it wasn't from Jackson since she had that conversation open and nothing new appeared. The little word balloon icon popped into the top bar. She tapped the button to go back to the list of names and saw Derek Davis in bold. An unread text awaited her.

DEREK DAVIS: I'm sorry about ruining your dinner. Have to sit through this company meeting. Should be done in an hour. Hope to see you after but if not I understand.

Farrah needed to clear her mind. She ran a brush through her hair and changed into comfortable, baggy cargo pants with layers of shirts. It felt as close to pajamas as she could get while still be dressed. She wasn't concerned with appealing to anyone's fashion sense on the eve of her shameful exit from the premises.

Thirty minutes were killed mostly because her actions were practically in slow motion. The soreness made her sluggish. Thinking of Derek, though, released the feel-good hormones. She headed to the restaurant bar figuring if she could eat something and get one cocktail into her, her nerves would settle. She was right.

A plate of hummus and what was probably six pitas cut up, filled her belly and took care of one of her issues. The hunger was gone. The Cosmo had something to absorb it so she wasn't snockered by the time Derek arrived.

When he did, his hand landed on the back of her barstool in such a way that his arm enclosed her. He stood close at first for a minute or two before finally sitting down.

"I'm glad you replied." He held up a couple fingers to get the bartender's attention. A local craft beer, nothing too pretentious.

"I almost didn't."

As they sat, their knees touched and bodies were swiveled toward each other. Even with their arms resting on the bar and fingers toying with their glasses, they managed to get their hands to graze each other. She stared at their hands rather than looking him in the eye. She felt like the trembling inside her had to be visible and wondered how he could sit next to such a flaky person.

He told her that he didn't want her to leave. She listened and continued to look anywhere but at him. He wasn't rambling, but he did feel obligated to fill the silence since she wasn't ready to talk.

"Brad reminded everyone about smart things to do regarding the hackers like changing passwords and that kind of crap. He also emphasized that no one should speak to reporters and if asked, we should direct them to our PR department."

The first Cosmo helped a little. She needed more courage to speak and held up her empty martini glass for the bartender to see. Clearly this was an experienced barkeep who knew to leave couples alone when it looked like they needed privacy.

Other Caressa Lamour staff that had taken up stools weren't speaking so quietly and weren't completely engrossed in each other. Derek seemed a little nervous when someone from the company looked over at them. Gossip would spread in no time how Derek sealed the deal with some disgraced massage therapist accused of sending their CEO to his grave.

"Derek, you know I'm married, right?"

"Yeah, I know. I'm not proud of being this jerk coming on to you. That's not how I am. I'm no saint, but while I was married, I was faithful."

"So you understand how difficult this is for me to spend this time with you. It's not like anything has happened or even will happen, but something is going on here."

"I know it's hard. I really do. But I'm relieved to hear that you feel these sparks too. I wasn't sure if it was all in my head."

"It's definitely not."

He ordered another beer, but she declined a third cocktail. Her phone buzzed. She was annoyed by the sudden disruption, but then saw it was from Samantha.

"I'm sorry. I need a minute to read this. I emailed the owner of our spa about the accusations by Chloe that we were violating the contract for services."

"Take your time."

Sam's response was exactly what Farrah needed. She said her legal counsel advised that they don't leave the premises because he was able to get through to Caressa Lamour. They came to an agreement that the spa would be compensated for the exact amount of work that Farrah was able to do, plus the hourly cost for an administrative assistant, meaning June.

"I don't know why on Earth your company thought they'd have to pay for the two practitioners that couldn't be here. That was never the case! Chloe made us sound like crooks ripping you off. The invoice would be for the expenses accrued by me and June and an accurate listing of how many one-hour full body massages, Mary's singular ninety-minute session, and all the fifteen minute chair massages I did. Nothing more!"

"That's great news, right? You can stay and keep working?"

"It sounds like it. Honestly, I have zero desire to work on anyone else here, but I need this money. My practice hasn't exactly taken off."

She typed out a reply to Samantha agreeing to the terms. The invoice with all the information would be sent to the HR department no later than seven days after the end of the retreat on Friday.

"It won't even take me seven days. June has been keeping meticulous records. It's a few clicks to make an invoice and email it."

"You better let June know not to pack."

She smiled at him finally. Her hands continued to hold onto the phone, but for several seconds she selfishly looked into his eyes and savored it before resuming her messages.

It was late and the November lack of daylight meant it was pitch black outside. When Derek suggested taking a walk in the cold, Farrah asked if there was somewhere else they could go. They ended up in the solarium where the morning yoga classes were held.

Derek's hands searched along the wall for a light switch. He found a panel with a series of dimmers and created the sort of glow that Farrah's eyes were used to during her private therapeutic sessions. She wondered who he was messaging when he took his phone out and used one thumb to click around. It wasn't a text though. The luscious sound of Billie Holiday's voice melted through the air. He laid the phone on an end table and took her hands in his.

"Dance with me."

She held his right hand and pressed her body against his, swaying slowly to the rhythms. It didn't matter whether they were in step with the music or not. She rested her cheek against his chest and closed her eyes. She felt his other hand at the small of her back pulling her closer. His hand ran along the waistline of her pants. Her skin got goosebumps underneath all the fabric. His fingers explored the space above her back pocket waiting for any sign whether they should stop. She didn't pull away. Her own hand drifted to the back to his hip telling him she wanted to touch him just as badly. He directed his hand further and cupped her ass delicately so as to not scare or offend her.

The two minutes of "You Go to My Head" was far too short. She lifted her head and looked at him in the soft light. The next song began and Farrah didn't for one second want to stop dancing with him other than to do things she shouldn't. Her lips parts slightly to give her extra oxygen. Everything about that moment felt surreal.

"I want to kiss you so badly," he said.

"I want you to."

They leaned even more into each other for a kiss that drove Farrah wild. Her hesitation was completely gone. She pretended something good in her life could be real. She desperately yearned to be desired just as much as she wanted him.

She didn't realize that while they swayed, they meandered close to a raised planter box filled with small trees, Michaelmas daisies, and herbs native to the region. Farrah was backed up against the edge of the wood where her butt pressed into the pine ledge. Before she knew it, Derek's hands slid down the back of her thighs and lifted her up so she was sitting. Her hands reached for stability and crushed the bed of stellaria that carpeted the soil around the other plants.

Her breathing got heavier with each kiss on her neck. One of his hands fondled her breast sending another wave of excitement through her. Her hips rocked and she could feel how hard he was through his jeans.

Farrah knew what to do as far as the mechanics of making out and heavy petting, but she felt stunted and unsure. She didn't have enough vodka to completely remove all the self-doubt though it helped enough to get her that far.

She shifted the right amount so that the thick seam of her own pants rubbed where she wanted it to. She knew they were in public, but they arrived at the moment where she let go of the control and moaned with each thrust hoping no one would pass through the side hallway leading to that room.

She forgot dry humping through clothes didn't exactly mean staying dry. It was fun and it felt great. She didn't care anymore about obligations, responsibilities, legal troubles, or whether Milton Byron was murdered. All that mattered was how Derek made her feel.

When Etta James sang "Something's Got a Hold on Me," Farrah could have sworn truer words had not been sung at just the right moment ever before in the history of music.

"Come back to my room," he said into her ear while she was clawing at his shirt trying to figure out how to slip her hands underneath it.

CHAPTER TWENTY-TWO

IN the morning, Farrah sat in the living room area of their suite sipping grotesque hotel room coffee waiting for June to come out so they could go get a proper breakfast.

"Morning." June's hair was a mess and covered half her face as she spoke. "What's the latest word from Samantha about whether you can work today?"

"Hey. The last email from her said I need to find Chloe and confirm so we can resume our schedule. Other than that, the airport finally set up cots and charging stations for all the people there. They're running on generators, but I guess it could be a lot worse." Farrah took another sip and it made her cringe. She put the mug down on an end table and tried to keep from nervously drinking from it.

June's oversized shirt probably belonged to her ex-husband or an ex-boyfriend. She wasn't wearing much else and she looked beautiful. She also wasn't hungover like Farrah was.

"Damn, girl, are those bags under your eyes or did you forget to take off your mascara?"

"Oh. I guess I had too many Cosmos last night at the restaurant."

"So you did go out. With Derek, I assume?"

"Yes, he was there. As were about seventy other employees from the company."

"Uh huh."

Farrah already had the laptop opened up to a browser window with tabs opened to the biggest social networks. Even though June set her up on several of them for business promotions, there were only two she cared about for personal interactions. The cushions of the loveseat bounced as June flopped next to her.

"What do we have here?" June peeked to see the screen and raised her eyebrows. "Doing some investigating on your new boyfriend?"

The screen was on Derek Davis' profile. Like she was a kid with her hand caught in the cookie jar, Farrah closed the laptop.

"No, come on! Let me see!" June took the computer from her and began to read through some of the information. "Divorced. Lives in Lambertville… nice. Oh and look… all the photos are of him rock climbing and playing sports. Shit, what's this?" June pointed to the photo album where Derek was in shorts and shirtless outside.

"He's hot. I know."

"No, you idiot. This!"

Farrah realized she never mentioned Derek's prosthetic leg to June. It's not that she was accustomed to seeing it, but she worked hard to train her mind into accepting bodies of all sizes, shapes, colors, and abilities. Somehow, she still managed to get almost exclusively fit women under 45 as clients and often pregnant, but it only took a couple months for her to see bodies in a new light.

"Oh, you didn't realize that either? Even when he rappelled down the cliff? We're terrible sleuths."

"What was it like?"

Farrah dodged the question and steered back to the information on his pages.

"It looks like these pictures were taken at a different company event. All these people tagged are people I've seen here this week. Look, there's Sagari Palla and Chloe Griffin and that skittish IT guy Micah.

Farrah clicked to open new tabs for different people she recognized. Not all of them listed their employer or where they lived. Most had their relationship statuses visible. Some shared seemingly every detail about their lives while others only posted memes.

"Hey, check to see if any of these people have BARN, animal rights, or vegetarian cuisine in their Likes list." June pointed to the part of the screen that showed Chloe's favorite movies, shows, music and books. Then there were places she checked in and finally the miscellaneous Likes which had hobbies, products, and other random things.

"Wow, look at the differences. Sagari is vegetarian and likes this anti-fur campaign. Meanwhile, Chloe likes these couture designers who use fur and crocodile leather and has several check-ins at a steakhouse." Farrah clicked through the other employees to keep snooping.

"If Chloe doesn't care about animals, does that mean she's off our suspect list?"

"That depends. Is the animal testing the reason Milton was pushed to his death?"

June fished through Farrah's attaché for a notebook and pen. She drew lines to make columns and put names down the list. Across the top for column headers she wrote: animal rights, hated Milton, worried about layoffs, and had opportunity.

"How are we going to fill in that last column? Everyone seemed to have the opportunity?"

"Not really. Remember what Mary said. Milton was supposed to have a breakfast meeting with Brad and Micah so those two should have been together waiting for him in the conference room." June wrote "no" in the last column for those two employees.

"I'm not sure we can assume that. What if they had their meeting and all of them went their separate ways? What if one of those guys was running late and wasn't there either? We need to find out where people were with our best estimation about when Milton was lured outside to the edge of the trail." Farrah watched June cross out the notations and they resumed snooping through the profiles. She scrolled through Sagari's timeline to read the updates.

"*Big changes coming*. I wonder what she meant by that," June said.

"That could mean anything. It could be about the layoffs or the change in the corporate structure."

June's finger targeted a spot on the post. "Look! This was posted the night before Milton died. Sunday night, when we got here."

"I'm not convinced that means anything. Not yet anyway. Let me try to find that former intern Whitney. If she was involved with BARN and the new CEO, I bet her profile is juicy."

They weren't disappointed. Whitney Gallagher's page read like a best-selling novel's outline. Over the past year, she went from happy and in love with posts about how wonderful her life was to angry. Really angry. Threatening to put an end to the powerful white male patriarchy that ruled over all living things. Calling the posts radical would be only tapping the surface. She didn't name names or the corporation. It was probably vague enough to keep her out of jail for terroristic threats.

"Go to her photos. I want to see if Brad is in any of them." June added Whitney's name to the list.

"There's a lot of people in them. Mostly selfies or group shots with her at rallies with other BARN activists."

"Keep going back. Back to when she was interning and happy."

They saw that Whitney and Brad had similar photos from some dinners, swanky business events, and a weekend getaway on a beach. Neither of them had blatant photos of them as a couple. Brad was in photos she took, but it showed him with people from the industry and even with celebrities hired to endorse the products.

Farrah double-checked Brad's "About" information. His relationship status wasn't filled in, or rather, if it was, it wasn't visible to people not on his friends list. Most of Brad's status updates were professional business posts linking to the corporate blogs or to articles related to the industry.

"Brad seems to have the strongest motive. With Milton out of the way, he's most likely to be chosen as the next CEO. He loved his work."

"He played a lot too as those beach and sports pictures show." June made some notes in the row for Brad. "Although who knows, maybe that was a business trip. The company seems to blend business and pleasure. I've heard sales reps get flown all over the world for rewards and for conferences where they put in two hours of work a day and basically have an all-expense paid vacation."

"Do you know who that celebrity is in the photos Whitney took of him?"

"She's not that famous. Not yet anyway. Her name is Lexi Peacock."

"Sounds like a role playing character." Farrah typed the name into a search bar. The results were bland. She didn't spot anything about animal rights.

"She's a soap opera star trying to break in to more respectable acting in movies and late night dramas."

"It's probably better that we narrow our list instead of add to it anyway."

June used her phone to help with the internet searches.

She found professional resume sites with tons of details about people. She tapped her way through Micah Maddox's links and discovered a user name associated with him on some controversial boards like Boost and ChanIA.

"Looks like your nerdy friend has some strong opinions on freedom of information and conspiracy theories."

"Who? Micah? Just tell me what you found." Farrah set aside the laptop to get herself water in place of the dreadful coffee.

"It's hard to sort it all out. They speak in a lot of shortened words, acronyms, and codes. Basically, I have no idea what he believes only that he's active on threads about hacking. I'd need time to search each of these topics to see what they're about."

"Well, we don't have time right now for that." Farrah picked up her phone and saw a new email. "I finally got that email from Chloe. We can get back to work as long as we charge them accurately for the two of us instead of the original plan."

June stood and folded her arms across her chest. "My money is on Brad Dubray. I think he had the most to gain by Milton's demise."

"I'm leaning towards the activists. I think someone in that group could easily be capable of violence and terrorism. We need to get ready though. I need to be in the massage room by nine so I guess we're skipping breakfast today."

Farrah showered and pulled her wet hair back into a bun like a ballerina. She put on a pair of scrubs and a t-shirt with "believe" in big letters.

June came out of her room wearing jeans and a comfortable rusty orange sweater accessorized with silver and turquoise jewelry.

"So, are we ever going to talk about last night and where you were?"

Farrah slipped her phone into a back pocket and picked up her tote bag. "Nope."

"Not ever or not now?"

"I need time. I don't want to keep anything from you. You know that."

June walked over to Farrah and hugged her.

"Look, I know I made my opinion on Derek known. I might not think getting involved with him is the best thing, but I'm here for you if you need to talk."

"I need to focus on work or I'll keep screwing things up."

They exited the room to head to their working suite, stopping for coffee in the dining hall on the way.

"Are you going to see him today?"

Farrah sipped from the paper cup. It was better than the swill before, but not great.

"Yes, I'm going to see him today."

CHAPTER TWENTY-THREE

FARRAH swiped the card to enter the massage suite. She flicked the light switch and put her coffee cup on the desk. June followed her in, opened the laptop, and started getting ready for the first client.

"You have four hours straight and then the rest of the day off."

"Without a break? What happened to the nice reasonable schedule you were organizing for me?" Farrah walked to the private room and dropped off her tote forcing June to speak louder.

"It's not my fault we missed breakfast. Besides, I believe in you. You can do this marathon and then rest up until tomorrow which will be our last day…" her voice faded.

"What?" Farrah came back to the main room clipping a holster around her waist for the cream jar. She took out an emery board out of one of the holsters and filed any potential hard edges of her fingernails.

"Nothing. I was describing our week working here in poetic language."

Farrah's body felt the toll of the rigorous hours she put in already. She thought about the night before and considered some of her aches and pains could have been from that too.

"The first woman emailed," June spun the computer around so Farrah could see it. "She wanted to make sure it was still okay for her to come in for the hour because she's having pain in her shoulder from bursitis. She normally sees a physical therapist."

"Did you tell her it was fine for her to come in?"

"I did. I don't even know if you can help her shoulder, but I figured if you couldn't, you could do something else like give her a foot massage and aromatherapy session."

"Good thinking, but yes, I can try to help her shoulder. Normally I'd give her an ice pack, but I didn't pack any of the hot and cold stuff for this trip." Farrah finished the coffee and rummaged for mints in the attaché on the desk. "I hope no disasters happen today."

Gracie Banks entered the suite. Farrah was used to giving assessments without even telling people what she was doing. This girl was young, much younger than people who complain about bursitis or arthritis unless they grew up with chronic medical issues. Farrah helped Gracie with an oversized bag that weighed six pounds easily; it was overkill to carry more than a wallet, cell phone, and maybe a bottle of water when going from one lodge room to another. This kid carried the important things in her life with her, probably all the time.

"Let me help you with that. We can keep it in the other room, but you don't need to carry so much when you're in pain already."

June asked Gracie to sign the client sheet and Farrah wasted no time escorting her to the other room.

"So tell me, what is an average day for you like? I like to understand the physical routines of my clients."

"Well, I could either be sitting at a desk all day or I could be mobile. It really depends on the day. I run one of the Twitter accounts for the company, but I'm mainly responsible for things like Instagram, SnapChat, Pinterest, Facebook - you know. Things that highlight photos of products."

"That sounds exciting." Farrah had no real understanding of what she was talking about.

"I get to travel a lot, so that's cool. I meet the celebrities and magazine editors. That sort of thing. But mainly, my job is to show off the stuff and the people who endorse it and keep myself invisible."

Farrah explained to Gracie the plan and how to get on the table. She left the room for two minutes. Before returning, she whispered to June.

"Hey. Did you check all the social feeds for Caressa Lamour? There's a ton of them and that girl is responsible for most of it."

"You mean Instagram and all that? Yes, I've checked. They have hundreds of hateful comments on every product. People calling them bunny killers. It gets gruesome. I'd rather not look at it anymore if it's all the same to you."

"But I need you to. See if any of those commenters can be traced back to the protesters who were here. If the comments are that serious, there's no reason we should dismiss someone's hate of this company and its CEO."

Back inside the darkened room, Farrah saw how skeletal Gracie's figure was. If she wasn't suffering from any other disease like cancer or thyroid problems, she was most likely abusing her body through eating disorders. Farrah wanted to talk to her about it, but it wasn't part of her agenda. She wasn't taking full medical histories on the clients at the conference. The only thing Gracie freely discussed with her was the pain in her shoulder. She barely had any muscle meat on her to be massaged. Farrah's hands felt like they were holding fistfuls of bones. She played out an entire feminist lecture in her head where she informed Gracie about the dangers of eating disorders and how she shouldn't buckle under the pressure of the beauty industry. She wanted to say so many things, but stayed silent.

After several minutes, the thoughts still hadn't settled down. What if that was her own daughter? Wouldn't she want a medical professional to give her the information or at least ask her if she wanted to talk? It became too difficult to see this girl probably only a year older than her daughter made into exactly what the media wanted which they would then continue to judge anyway.

She picked up one of Gracie's hands and used the pads of her thumbs to work in circles on the girl's palm. "Now, Gracie, I want you to think of this place as your safe space for as long as you're here. Each time you exhale, a little more pressure that's been building up will release. You inhale and feel revitalized and refreshed. You exhale and let go."

After three rounds of deep breathing, Gracie started to cry. Farrah assured her everything was going to be fine. She kept a hand on Gracie's arm while she reached for a tissue from the box on the credenza.

"I'm sorry. I'm not an emotional person. I've never been. But this week - with all those people online attacking the company - well, it's hard not to take it personally when I'm the one that has to read every single comment, ya know?"

"Of course. You're safe here. You can vent all you like. This is your time." Farrah took the snotty tissue and replaced it with a clean one.

The tears stopped quickly. Gracie had more stamina than Farrah expected.

"Those damn BARN people! They're lunatics. You know that, right? They have their own scandals. I've read the investigations against them. They go around preaching about saving animals, but I read that they put down ninety-seven percent of the animals they 'rescued' last year." Gracie air-quoted for emphasis. "I wish we didn't test on animals. Trust me. But I can't do anything about it. My job is to show off shiny new bottles and colors and get people to believe Photoshopped actresses really use our stuff."

Gracie got everything out of her system, it seemed. She was under a lot of stress managing the digital footprint of the company, but she didn't open up about her body issues or mention those magic words: "being out of control." When Gracie was leaving, Farrah gave her a business card and told her that she would gladly schedule stress management and relaxation appointments with her if she could get to Riverside Wellness Spa.

June ran down the list of people scheduled. She had a couple of half hour back massages that would be done on the table in the private room instead of the chair in public. Then she had a full body pre-natal session which was something she couldn't seem to escape in her work at the spa.

The last session was someone named Arleana Armistead who finally presented Farrah with something different instead of the common one hour Swedish massage. This woman requested some of her time to be spent in a guided meditation and the rest doing assisted stretches for her tight muscles because she loved to run obstacle courses. Farrah couldn't wait for that session. It would be easier on her own body and it would break her boring routine. A win-win situation, as far as she was concerned.

Between Hasan Doda, the second short session, and Regan Leonetti, the pregnant woman, Farrah begged June for a break.

"I did the best I could going through all those comments, but honestly, it's time consuming. User names on threatening messages aren't usually going to have the same user name as someone's professional or personal profile. They make fake accounts to post this garbage."

A woman lumbered into the makeshift waiting room and leaned her heavy rotund body against June's desk. She was out of breath and looked like she hadn't slept in a week.

"I'm Regan Leonetti. I have an appointment, but I need to pee already. Can I use your bathroom?"

"Of course. It's right over there." Farrah stood and pointed the way, much to the displeasure of her aching feet and back.

With the client out of earshot, June brought up the sensitive subject of Derek.

Farrah whispered. "I don't know what it all means. I don't know how I feel about him."

"He's a stranger, Farrah. Don't throw away what you have because you're in a rough patch."

"Dammit, June. You contradict yourself every day. Half the time, you're urging me to leave Jackson to live with you."

"And I still want that. I think that's the best thing. But I also don't want you throwing something away because of some hot guy."

"You're my best friend even though you're a raging pain in the ass sometimes. I'm not going to stop being friends with you because of some random guy. I haven't walked away from our friendship even when my husband wanted me to."

"I'm sorry, sweetie. I'm being a jerk. I shouldn't tell you what to do."

The toilet flushed and the sounds of the sink broke their soft spoken yet heated exchange. Farrah managed to get through the two final appointments of the day without incident.

It wasn't anger that she harbored against June. She couldn't identify it. The more she thought about June's warnings, the more she realized it was herself that should be the target of her pent up feelings. She was the one responsible for her actions including her share of the responsibility in her failed marriage. June was her saving grace.

They didn't talk about Derek on the way back to their suite. Once inside, Farrah collapsed on the loveseat and left her legs dangling over the arm.

She let her younger self down. The Farrah from ten, fifteen, or twenty years ago that had ambitions, was madly in love, and spent her time raising a great kid. She hated the part of herself that found all that boring and steered her from one bad decision to the next.

CHAPTER TWENTY-FOUR

THE text alert vibrated Farrah's phone in her back pocket. It couldn't have been June so she guessed it was Derek asking about seeing her.

"He wants me to go for a walk with him."

"Something rubs me the wrong way about him. I don't know what it is, but please be careful."

"I'll text you on a regular basis just to say I'm okay."

"Fair enough. Meanwhile, he's still on my snooping list so I'll be Googling the shit out of him while you're gone."

Farrah was relieved to see June's snarky attitude back in place. She much preferred that over June's jealousy and insecurity. If Farrah could will herself to be pansexual, she would, but she couldn't. She loved June and never denied a low level of physical attraction, but not enough to keep someone satisfied in a relationship. She loved a strong man between her legs. She once heard a sex educator refer to top-only girl to girl interest as "boobiesexual" and that seemed to fit her fine.

The hot water in the tub turned her skin lobster red. If Derek expected her to walk even a half mile, she needed to loosen up. The bath salt released a blend of citrus, basil, peppermint, cardamom, with a hint of cinnamon. The bath salts were definitely not tested on animals. They were made by one of Farrah's massage school classmates who decided to launch a small business making products instead of practicing bodywork. Like the mass produced cosmetics, Farrah still couldn't be certain of the raw materials.

As dangerous as it was, she kept her phone on a dry washcloth on the floor next to the tub so it could be in arm's length. She ignored the first couple buzzes and focused on letting her legs and arms float in the water. By the third buzz, relaxation escaped her. She dried off her hands, leaned over the side, and checked the messages.

June left texts which said she was taking the laptop to the seating area by the massive fireplace where she planned to sip on hot cocoa laced with Irish whiskey. When Farrah didn't reply with a simple "OK" to her, she got cocky with ridiculous nonsense.

JUNE CHO: I'm gonna get liquored
up, seduce that Chloe bitch and
break her heart

JUNE CHO: srsly did you drown in
there?

Farrah let her know she approved of June's ludicrous
fantasy to seduce the nasty HR manager who kept trying to make
her professional life hell.

FARRAH WETHERS: I'd like to
push her off a cliff.

Farrah grunted after her fingers tapped that out and typed
out a well-meaning confession of regret.

FARRAH WETHERS: sry that was
so wrong. Bad karma.

Even though her midday bath had succeeded in reducing
some muscle tension, it was time to get out and get dressed. The
knocking on the door shot directly to Farrah's heartbeat,

speeding it up. She denied him when he asked to come in and suggested they get their walk started.

The Shawnee Conference Center and Resort property wasn't all lakefront. Derek lead Farrah along some trails that passed the recreational activity areas that most people used for fun, but corporations would use for their team building exercises. Farrah was more familiar than she wanted to be with the rock climbing area, but the other courses, she was excited to see.

He took her passed the fence obstacles where three fences of different heights needed to be climbed over. The easiest one was six feet tall with small wooden shims for people to use much like the fake rock climbing that's done indoors in city gyms. The second one was even higher with the shims further apart. The ten foot wall only had a few shims. That's where more teamwork was necessary for people to boost each other; sometimes one person stayed at the top to give a helping hand.

The next spot he took her to had a small creek leading to the lake. The water was clear and cold. Snakes, frogs, and newts could have been hidden by any of the rocks.

"This is my favorite."

There was a series of logs mounted on pillars. The bravest warrior teams took the highest log. During the training, thick mats were transported from the closest supply cabin and laid under the logs. Then two people would stand on the opposite ends of the log and cross to the other side. To make it progressively more complicated, they had to carry different objects varying from small and heavy to large but light. The goal was to navigate around each other at the middle without either person falling or dropping their cargo. The learning experience observed by employers was to see who thought more about their own safety than the other person and who put material items in front of human safety. The latter could have been what mega corporations preferred. Farrah didn't wage any assumptions out loud to her companion.

"And you don't have any problems with all these climbing and balancing challenges?"

"I wondered when you were going to ask about my leg."

"You don't have to say anything. I'm curious about it from a physiology standpoint. I'm interested to know about different bodies and how people function in their lives."

"I function very well, Farrah, as you may have noticed." He winked. She took that as a sign that he wasn't offended.

"I know massage seems like some frou-frou spa therapy, but I honestly do approach my work with as much whole being and wellness information as I can. Now that I've seen what you can do, imagine how it will be if I have a client in the future who is missing a limb. I have experience with it now and I can try to make someone comfortable and more confident if they aren't already."

"You're pretty sweet. I hope all your clients know how special you are."

They passed the ropes course where he told her a trick he learned from watching videos of Navy SEAL training. The way to get up the rope was not to squeeze it between the thighs, but wrap it around one foot from the outside to the inside where the other foot locks it in place allowing for the climber to reach with their arms and pull up again, then repeat.

"Navy SEAL videos? You sure you weren't one before you lost your leg?"

"I wish. No. I've lived a boring life of college lacrosse and rowing, followed by grad school, and then corporate life ever since." The distant look on his face was easy for her read. She could tell he had some regrets in his life choices. Perhaps it was in not taking more risks or maybe choosing steady practical paychecks over adventure. There was something there in his eyes that silently spoke of longing.

Farrah realized thirty minutes had gone by since she last checked in with June. She gave another smart ass text.

FARRAH WETHERS: haven't
been kidnapped by hillbilly
cannibals, still alive.

June's message back distracted Farrah from whatever
Derek was saying:

JUNE CHO: Ask him where his ex
is. I found her name & kept
searching. There's no sign of her
anywhere after last year.

Farrah was uncomfortable by the thought of digging into
his personal life. Talking about his leg was hard enough. She
hoped he would open up of his own accord, but he had a way of
not saying anything specific unless she directly asked.

"Derek, I need to talk to you about something."

"Oh. Okay, I already know what you want to say."

"You do?"

"You're going to say that you're married and this was
nice for a few days, but it's a fantasy. And in two days, you need
to go back home to the real world with your husband and your
daughter."

"Well, yes. That's somewhat accurate. But I want to get to know you better too. And unfortunately, that does mean we talk about what went wrong in our marriages. You haven't said anything about yours except that you're divorced."

The path was obscured by all the fallen leaves. The smell of the earthly decay crept through Farrah's senses. A huge wolf spider web blocked their way. She felt creeped out by it and at the same time sad that the only way through was to destroy it.

"There's not much to tell, I'm afraid. Jennifer had her own ambitions. She wanted to leave and follow her own path. It was a path that would have meant me quitting my great job and moving to Europe. I didn't want to. We weren't in love enough for either of us to sacrifice our pursuits. It's quite simple. Our careers always came first."

Farrah had to step over a large cluster of thick roots. Her body didn't feel like giving it the hop over them that would have been faster. She balanced her right foot between a couple of knotty spots and propelled herself forward. Derek's longer gait didn't present the same obstacle. He effortlessly planted his artificial foot in its specially styled ankle boot and stepped over the woody tangles.

"What does she do for a living that was more important than being married to you?"

"She's a biologist."

Hello, feelings of inadequacy, Farrah thought. She was a feminist, but incredibly successful, intelligent women intimidated her. She forever felt like she didn't have the full potential those other women had. She didn't have the drive, the brain power, nor the money for such advanced education. Her one year in a trade school to start a new career had been a financial struggle that she paid for with retirement savings, a loan, and a grant.

"A scientist? Wow. That's interesting."

"We met at work actually. But she got an offer to transfer to the office in France, so she took it. Why do you keep texting? Enjoy the world in front of you."

Farrah hit the send button after cluing June into the facts. Jennifer was in France so perhaps the reason she couldn't find information on her was because she was busy living an extraordinary life far, far away and in another language. June said she didn't buy the story. She insisted that internet searches for ProKinect profiles should have returned something even if it was in another language that the browser would offer to translate no matter how poorly.

"I promised June that I'd check in often. After Milton plummeted over the side of a cliff and could've been there for hours suffering, she doesn't want me disappearing."

"But you're not alone like Milton was. I'm here. I'll make sure you don't have a terrible accident."

The excitement and goosebumps Farrah felt when he smiled and talked about someone falling to his death wasn't even close to the brand of excitement she felt when they were kissing in the solarium. What she felt was doubt in his authenticity.

CHAPTER TWENTY-FIVE

FARRAH was never one to ignore her anxiety. She figured if her body had a physical reaction to something, no matter how benign that thing was, she was meant to acknowledge it. Then she would determine if she had an appropriate reaction to a situation or if her mind had lied to her and made her feel like the world was ending when it really wasn't.

Nearing the end of the forest path, Farrah found herself in a position of uncertainty. For a few days, this strange man Derek seemed like the sort of person who had some philosophies she didn't appreciate, but overall, she would have labeled him as a Nice Guy. The problem is Nice Guys are often Dangerous Guys in disguise.

Derek Davis seemed to have it all: good looks, stamina, determination, perseverance during challenging times, and success even after failure. But what Farrah noticed were the moments of callousness that he'd accidentally show. He didn't seem particularly remorseful about Milton's death nor about his own divorce. It's not that Farrah believed employees needed to have a strong emotional bond to their superiors, but Milton's last moments of life were right before their eyes.

"Derek, this was fun and all, but I think I'd like to get back to June and spend some time with her that isn't working. She's really bailed me out this week and I don't want her to think I'm taking advantage of her."

"I'm disappointed in you, Farrah." He placed both hands on her hips and looked down into her eyes. "No, I take that back. I'm disappointed in me. I thought I was interesting enough for you."

She put a flat hand on his chest to try and make some distance between them, but it didn't work. He held her close.

"It's not a matter of finding you interesting, which of course I do. It's about being polite and caring to the greatest friend I've ever had. I'm sorry, but I think she and I need a girls' night."

Derek finally eased up and let his hands drop away from her. The early afternoon sunlight greeted them when they broke through the tree cover. They crossed the brown grass heading toward the building's lakeside entrance.

A few cliques of Caressa Lamour employees dotted the outdoor scenery. Closest to the back stairs and handicap ramp,

Farrah saw Gracie Banks, the social media expert. She was talking to Chloe Griffin in what appeared to be a tense exchange.

Chloe looked like she was cut from the pages of a Ralph Lauren catalog. Gracie was bundled up in so many intentionally mismatched layers topped with a crocheted beanie on her head that Farrah wondered which of them was really the trendsetter for the company.

"What do you know about Gracie? The young girl over there with Chloe."

Derek stopped on the second step and looked around to see what Farrah was talking about.

"I don't know her. I've seen her around, but I didn't even know her name."

"I would have thought people in sales would work closely with people from marketing and promotions."

"She probably answered to Brad before he got promoted or the director below him most likely."

"Isn't this conference supposed be about opening up lines of communication and building trust with the whole team?"

Derek huffed and smirked. "That's how they sell it to people. It's about rewarding the top performers with a week away from our desks and for the higher ups to observe who doesn't play well with others."

Chloe caught sight of Farrah watching them. She ended her conversation with Gracie and they went separate ways. Gracie headed toward the back stairs where Farrah and Derek still lingered. She stared at her phone as if the rest of the world around her didn't exist. Farrah was surprised she looked up at all to say, "Hi," in a way that lacked all emotional resonance.

"I guess some people will never take time to enjoy a view like this." Farrah maintained her distance physically from Derek while she looked out at the lake and mountains.

He took a step up to be closer to her. "Not me." He looked at her rather than nature.

For that moment, she found herself enraptured by him all over again. There was no space between them. He blocked the way down the stairs by having his hand on the railing. He didn't trap her exactly - she noticed. If she wanted to, she could have finished going up the other side of the stairs to the spacious veranda. But that's not what she did. She stood still and felt her blood warm up her body. She felt the way she did the night they kissed. If he was dangerous, it was something her body found arousing. Their lips were so close she could feel his breath on her face.

"You know where to find me if you change your mind about tonight." He left her hanging there without the kiss she craved. He went back down the two steps and walked backwards away from her until he finally pivoted and headed west where the pool building wasn't far away.

Farrah's inner voices screamed at her for the continuous urges that made her feel out of control. She wanted to want to keep her hands and lips to herself. The problem was that she felt like she was never going to be able to say no to him. She let things go too far already. When she thought she could back on track, she found him too hard to resist. Had he hypnotized her somehow? She couldn't blame alcohol all the time. He certainly hadn't drugged her because she remembered every single thing they did together.

"Where have you been?" June looked up from the comfort of the plush chair in front of the fire place. Farrah found her in the seating area with the carnage of pastries, hot cocoa, and whiskey next to her on the maple end table.

"I was giving my liver a rest and went out for fresh air and exercise." Farrah took the seat on the other side of the small table. She kept sipping on the eco-conscious refillable bottle of water she carried around. "I'm starving. Did you eat?"

"I did, but I could eat more. You know that." June's great genetics kept her looking fit and healthy even though she endlessly dumped garbage into her body. "I'm in the middle of something though. Can you grab us some sandwiches and come back here?"

Farrah agreed. She went back to her room first for a pit stop. She traded her jacket for lighter yet still toasty warm blue flannel shirt with a moose on the breast pocket. She looked down and felt how worn the fabric was. It was a shirt she commandeered from Jackson many years before.

She returned to the cozy nook with veggie paninis for them to snack on. June took her plate and swapped it for the laptop. Farrah had no other option than to put her plate on the table and see what cyber antics June was up to.

"You've been chatting with Whitney this whole time?" Farrah kept her voice low in case Caressa Lamour staff in the area could overhear them.

"I kept in touch with her after I brought her to security. I felt bad for her. I know she's caught up with those nutjobs, but she seems like a good person. Her heart was in the right place. And I can't help but have sympathy for her after she slept with her boss and he ghosted on her."

Farrah waited for some people to walk passed behind their seats before continuing. She took a couple bites, savoring the roasted garlic olive oil. "She say anything good?"

"She's the one that gave me the idea to look up Derek's ex-wife. Maybe she has an active imagination, but maybe she's observant and it gets her into trouble. She told me Dr. Jennifer Singer disappeared and was never heard from again."

"Oh that's nonsense. His ex-wife got a promotion and transferred to the headquarters office in Europe. There's nothing suspicious about it."

June finished her sandwich then studied the remainder of the no longer hot cocoa in the mug. "If it's not suspicious, then why isn't there any sign of her?"

"I have no idea. Maybe her work is so classified the company doesn't allow her to be online."

"It's cosmetics, sweetie, not CERN."

"CERN is in Switzerland, not France."

"Whatever."

Farrah wanted to get back to the subject of Whitney Gallagher. She was likely in a ton of trouble legally for leaking the video to BARN since her whistleblowing wasn't done through appropriate channels. June didn't know much, only that BARN was asked to provide a lawyer for her. They didn't jump at the chance. But if they didn't, Whitney's plan was to set up a crowdfunding account to cover her defense.

"She mostly talked about Brad and her broken heart."

"What do you think he got out of that relationship?" Farrah longed for something more potent than the lemonade she picked up to go with her lunch. She knew saving any chance at being tipsy was best left for dinner or later when most of the people at the lodge would be doing the same thing.

"Other than a nubile piece of ass? I don't know. I'm sure it made his ego bigger - among other things. Probably made him feel younger too. At a certain point, you don't want to be reminded that you're aging. I can't imagine they had anything substantial in common."

"He got laid and she got to believe they were in love? That's it? God, I hate men sometimes."

"Sing it, sister." June pulled the laptop back and put it on the table between them. She navigated to a different browser tab to show Farrah something she found intriguing.

"Besides Whitney, did you know someone else was connected to BARN?"

"June, that's what we've been trying to figure out. Who did you find?"

"Pay attention - this requires some thinking. Remember that woman Sandra you worked on?"

"The gorgeous one? Sure."

"Before becoming an account manager for Caressa Lamour, she worked for four years at an ad agency. And before that, she worked in a department store in New York City which was when she volunteered for an animal shelter doing all their graphic design and brochures, things like that."

"Not all shelters are connected to BARN."

"No, but it's something. It's the best lead I found. Tons

of people post cute pet photos or share links of animals that need homes, like after so many were displaced from the hurricane. But this was the first employee I found besides Whitney that has actually volunteered for an animal organization."

"Good work, babe. Let me know if you find anything else. Are you still convinced Brad killed Milton now?"

"Our first night here, we saw two men arguing outside. I bet that was Brad and Milton. So, yeah, my money is still on Brad."

CHAPTER TWENTY-SIX

WEDNESDAY

THE ladies were more responsible about their night away from home. They had dinner alone without Derek tagging along making it uncomfortable. A couple glasses of wine and an early bedtime rounded it out for the best example of "adulting" they had accomplished since arriving.

One of the amenities Farrah and June hoped to take advantage of while at the Shawnee Conference Center and Resort was the indoor swimming pool. It was unfortunately not attached to the main building so in order to enjoy it, they had to bundle up for the fifty degree air outside before entering the steaminess of the mostly glass pool building.

It was so early, none of the Caressa Lamour employees were there. They had the whole place to themselves. There were daily team building activities in the pool on the Caressa Lamour schedule in the afternoons.

"I can't believe this company uses sports and competitive puzzle solving as a way to improve interpersonal relationships." June grabbed towels from a shelving unit they passed on the way to the locker room.

Most of the lights were off except for the hallway to the locker room and the lights in the pool illuminating it from under the water. Farrah thought it looked a bit magical, something a little frightening yet mesmerizing like a cove for mythical sirens.

"Competition drives business. I guess that means even competition between coworkers. I don't understand all of it. I tried playing on the Saint Sebastian softball team once and all it did was drive me further away from any of those people. They take it far too seriously. It's no fun." Farrah plopped her tote bag on the bench and started unbuttoning her flannel shirt.

"I can't imagine you playing softball." June sat and pulled off her favorite cowgirl boots. She managed to make them work with patterned leggings and a big brown sweater.

"I wanted to find a way to get exercise that wouldn't bore me, but I hated every second of being there. Definitely not my thing." Farrah pulled on her modest one piece bathing suit and still felt self-conscious about her body's jiggling spots and the unkempt bikini-scaping job she did. "Thank god no one is here."

June looked at her friend's bikini line. "I guess you didn't mind Derek seeing an unwaxed bush?"

"Stop."

"You're lucky. Natural is back in."

Farrah wasn't much of a swimmer. She drifted around the shallow end and worked on holding her breath. June swam laps lengthwise across the pool but far more casually than someone interested in form, toning, or calorie burning. Her braided long black hair looked like a sea snake under the water.

Both women left a towel and their phones on chairs along the bank of windows having secured the rest of their clothes in the locker room. The distinctive ringtone from Farrah's phone cut through the sound of swishing water. She pulled herself out at the edge closest to the chair instead of going over to the stairs.

"It's Jackson. I better take this." She wiped her hands on the towel and swiped open the phone. She continued to dry off one-handed and walked away toward the locker room for privacy. She would tell June everything discussed, but that was different than subjecting her to a potential fight. At the rate their conversations were going, Farrah knew arguing was more likely to happen than any kind of pleasant exchange.

"Which bank?" she said as she rounded the darkness into the light of the distant hallway.

June resumed her swimming. She spun around for a meandering backstroke that brought her into the shallow end. She spread her arms along the cement edge at the corner and let her legs rise to the surface.

In the locker room, Farrah listened as Jackson told her one of their banks express mailed new cards to them.

"We have new account numbers now and the new style cards with chips in them."

"What about the checking accounts?"

"They said that will take probably until the end of today to unfreeze. I admit I lost my cool with someone on the phone, but I'm furious."

"They're only trying to protect themselves and our money, hopefully. But I'm with you on this. I wish they weren't keeping us from our own funds." She used her elbow to hold the towel in place and wrapped it around herself with her free hand.

"And the dog needs to go back to the vet."

Gordon was old and had some typical problems that came with aging. Farrah didn't want him in pain if that was a problem, but some of the things Jackson took him to the vet for were the equivalent of taking a kid to the emergency room for a paper cut.

Fortunately, Jackson and Gordon were at home and the reporters long since moved on to some other prey.

"When are you coming home?"

She was surprised he was interested in her return. The absence of the press camped out on their lawn must have eased up his grumpy mood.

"I think we'll be leaving here Friday around one. Depends on whether we stay for lunch or if someone begs for appointments."

"But you got that contract situation taken care of, right?"

"Yes. They'll be paying the spa for my time and expenses despite being shorted two practitioners."

After the relatively cordial conversation ended, Farrah tapped the red button. She rested for a moment to acknowledge and enjoy the fact that they managed to talk without raised voices.

The splashing she heard perked her up. June must have changed her casual laps to something erratic. Farrah head back to the pool area to find the most horrifying scene she could imagine.

Someone in a hooded sweatshirt was holding June under the water while her arms flailed at the surface.

"Hey! Stop!" Farrah ran as fast as she could, dropping the towel, and hoping not to slip.

The frightening figure immediately bolted out the door leaving June's body grotesquely spotlighted by the underwater lamps. Farrah jumped in, grabbed June's arm, and pulled her body close to her. Luckily it was the shallow end so all she had to do was get to her feet and both of them had heads above water. She pulled her friend to the steps and sat at the top with June's body supported by her lap.

"Come on! Come on! Come on! Don't do this!" Farrah cradled June's head in the crook of her arm and flipped her to one side. She patted her back as hard as she could.

The coughing, choking, and wheezing were the greatest sounds Farrah ever heard.

"Thankyouthankyouthankyou," she said to any spirit that would listen. She pulled June up as far out of the water as she could.

June was confused and held on to Farrah for support.

"What the hell happened?"

"Someone tried to kill you. That's what happened." She held her and didn't want to let go.

June pulled back to look around the room, not that she would see the culprit who was long since out the door.

"All I remember is that I was hanging on to the side. I had my eyes closed. I didn't hear anything. And then these hands pushed me under. I popped up once, but my foot slipped on the bottom and I smacked the back of my head. And he kept me pushed down. It was the scariest thing in my life."

"For me too. I'm just glad he ran off so I could get to you in time."

"Thank you for that. You could've gone after him and assumed I was already dead."

"You're not dying. Not now anyway."

They got out of the water all together and sat on the chair where Farrah previously had her phone and towel. She kept an arm around June, too afraid to let go of her.

"Are you sure it was a man? I didn't get a good look. He or she took off as soon as I yelled."

"I'm not sure. It felt like big hands, but that doesn't mean anything."

"Maybe we should give up. This retreat has been nothing but one disaster after another. I'm through. I'm done. I can't stand it anymore and want to get our asses home where it's safe."

June tried to assure Farrah that she was fine. She suggested they immediately get dressed and call the police though to get it on record. Farrah insisted on being the one to make the call which she followed up with a call to Markos, the guy who had promised everyone the lodge was safe.

They agreed to wait for Sergeant Caldwell in the pool building, but they dried off and got dressed. Markos wasn't on site either. Caldwell showed up first and Markos arrived fifteen minutes later making them repeat everything.

"This whole retreat for Caressa Lamour was organized by Chloe Griffin. She's the contact I had on file." Markos put his pen back into his breast pocket and closed his notebook mirroring the moves of Caldwell. "I suggest you get in touch with her right away. I'll call her too, but I'm sure she'll want to hear from you and make sure you're both okay."

"It has nothing to do with whether we're okay and everything to do with whether Ms. Cho and I will sue Caressa Lamour and this conference center. You clearly have no idea how to keep people safe here!"

June rested her head on Farrah's shoulder and they kept their arms wrapped around each other.

"Let's get back to our room. Hopefully no one will try to murder us there." June's delivery could barely be called sarcasm by that point.

Markos went to his office and made the call to Chloe while Caldwell escorted the women back to their suite. He instructed them to stay locked in and not let anyone in except for himself or Markos. Not even any of the other conference center employees who may want to check on them once word spread.

"You should call Samantha and tell her this place should be shut down and that we should leave with full pay." June wasn't messing around. Now that her life was on the line, she wasn't going to play along with Caressa Lamour's stupid revised contract and NDA. "I'm calling my divorce lawyer to see if she can recommend someone to cover my ass in this."

"That's a great idea. I'll go in on that with you. If you're in danger, I'm sure I am too. I want someone to contact them and explain adamantly that we are done here and not fulfilling our end of the contract." Farrah was already dialing the phone to call Samantha. She texted Jackson right after.

"Do you care if Jackson tells Frank? I mean, they are close."

"Just because my ex and I don't hate each other and can manage to be in the same room that does not make us friends. It's none of his business, but I don't care what Jackson tells him. I'm not about to. That's for sure." June gave into her need for a distraction and opened the laptop to see what people were posting.

"Hopefully the lawyer will call us back soon and we can pack up." Farrah debated whether to text Derek or not. Would he care? She didn't know if he had real feelings for her or if she was a conquest to him. Word would no doubt get around among the Caressa Lamour people. Things only stay secret for so long.

"As soon as that lawyer calls back, I'm asking about whether I can leak this online and to the press. This whole thing needs to be shut down and they need to admit that Milton Byron was murdered."

"I agree with you this time. I'm not interested in protecting the privacy of people like Chloe Griffin or Brad Dubray. Screw them." Farrah decided not to text Derek after all. She went to shower off the chlorine and put comfortable clothes on.

CHAPTER TWENTY-SEVEN

FARRAH received a call from Chloe Griffin at nine that morning. She expected to hear from her sooner, but knowing that callous corporation, Chloe must have been on the phone with lawyers and executives before being able to call her.

"This retreat was supposed to be a way to reward our employees. We never anticipated violence from those animal rights people. You have our most sincere apologies."

Farrah pushed the speaker button and held the phone up for June to hear.

"Ms. Griffin, I emailed you the contact information for our lawyer."

"In light of these events, the company will consider a quiet settlement for your inconvenience."

"Being assaulted is more than an inconvenience." June didn't hold back. Her anger was not to be quelled this time.

Farrah and June could read each other's minds at that

point. A payoff from a huge corporation like Caressa Lamour would come with strings attached.

Farrah shook her head "no" hoping June understood she wanted her to be quiet for a minute. "We'll be sure to review it with our lawyer and the spa's owners. In the meantime, I'll be canceling the rest of the appointments your employees booked."

Neither of them could stand being locked up in their room against their wishes. They wanted food at the very least. June grabbed at her tiny waistline and suggested room service.

"We were told not to open the door for anyone." Farrah moved from the loveseat to the table and woke the laptop up from its sleep mode. June had left several browser tabs opened including the spa's software interface that they accessed over the web.

"I made sure we had everyone's cell numbers and room numbers if you want to start making the cancellation calls." June found the retreat center binder of services on a side table and rifled through to find a room service menu. "They're paying so how about one of everything?"

"Fine by me." Even though Farrah wouldn't eat any of the breakfast meats she still indulged in French toast and pancakes. "You better check with Markos first or better yet, make him deliver it personally."

"I like how you think."

Having a person nearly murdered on their premises after someone died mysteriously, the Shawnee staff reached new levels of ass kissing to accommodate requests. Markos came up with a list of approved employees who were allowed to visit the suite and essentially be at the beck and call of Farrah and June for the rest of their stay. Plus, Sergeant Caldwell ordered a patrol officer to stand guard at their door. It was awkward, but necessary.

"Derek keeps texting. I don't know what I should say. I keep telling him I'm busy and can't talk." Farrah caught herself calculating calories in her head while she stabbed at the pile of French toast and moved two pieces to her plate. They had fresh fruit, croissants, yogurt with granola, French toast, and pancakes spread out before them.

"He must know by now. They've had breakfast by now and one of their activities already. I mean, there's a cop at our door. I'm sure people have seen him standing there and started to gossip."

"I guess I can say something happened, but I'm not allowed to discuss it and assure him that we're both fine." Farrah gave into the stress and ate as much as she wanted. She wasn't burning any of it off, but having June alive and at her side mattered a lot more than dieting.

June picked up her phone when it chirped. "It's Frank. I guess Jackson told him."

"Are you going to answer it?"

"I'll get back to him." She sliced a croissant and filled it with scrambled eggs. "I have a ton of emails though that I've been ignoring. At least canceling the schedule means I can catch up with my real job and life."

"I'm so sorry for everything. I feel completely responsible." Farrah sat back from the temptation to continue gorging. "Don't you think that was awfully fast for Caressa Lamour to say they have a settlement?"

"I'm sure it's nothing. They aren't actually going to admit to any liability. It'll be peanuts like covering the full cost of the week but allowing us to leave early without finishing the work."

"I'm going to butt in here. You should text Frank back at the very least even if you don't feel like talking to him. It's nice of him to check on you."

"Sweetie, if you ever divorced, you'll see just how uncomfortable that is."

Divorce lingered through Farrah's mind almost every day. She didn't want to admit defeat, but she hadn't come up with any kind of solution to get them back on the same page. They grew apart. It happened all the time. She felt foolish for thinking she and Jackson were any different from the average couple. She most definitely did not want a man like Derek Davis to be the catalyst though.

"At this point, I don't think it's a matter of 'if' but 'when' we get divorced. I simply can't consider it while this job isn't making me enough money."

June cleared the plates and took possession of the laptop to do her own thing more efficiently than thumb-typing on her phone. She also posted an update to Farrah's social media accounts: "Due to an emergency, all appointments have been canceled for the rest of the week." She logged out of Farrah's accounts and opened her own.

"I don't care if I'm not allowed to talk about anything yet, but I have every right to let people in my life know I'm not dead." She updated her status to vaguely announce that she was fine but still not home. "I should be allowed to tell my real employer too. What if I start having trouble sleeping or need therapy? They'll need to approve time off."

"Wait to see what all these lawyers say. And you really should go see a doctor as soon as possible."

"I feel fine physically. I'm spooked and nervous, but I don't need the ER."

"Trust me as a professional when I say nerves and stress have physical effects. You need to see a doctor. A regular family doctor will do."

They stopped talking when they heard voices outside their door. Both got up and went over to listen. June looked through the peephole.

"It's Derek. The cop won't let him talk to us."

Derek called out Farrah's name loudly. She hoped he wasn't the type of alpha male to cause a scene and end up tackled by the cop.

She rested her hand on the door's handle and looked at June. "Do you feel safe enough if I open the door and tell him we're fine?"

"Go ahead. But he's not coming in."

Farrah held the door open the few inches that the safety catch allowed. Both the officer and Derek looked at the little bit of her face showing.

"Derek. Um. Hi."

"What's going on? Why is this cop here? He said I can't talk to you."

"Yeah, we had a bit of a situation this morning and we're not talking to anyone that hasn't been cleared by Markos Demisovski or Sergeant Caldwell."

The officer kept an arm across the threshold giving a physical barrier between him and Farrah. Derek could have tried to push through, but refrained.

"As long as you're all right. Can you text me at least?"

"Um. Not really. It's best if June and I keep to ourselves until we can leave. But we're fine now. In one piece. I swear."

"This is ridiculous. I'm sorry. I guess I'll leave you alone."

She thought he gave a sympathetic look before he waved and walked away. She thanked the officer for his intervention and then closed the door. She kept her hand pressed against the cold door as if that was somehow keeping it barricaded from intruders.

"I want to go home."

Farrah hadn't seen June this sad in a long time. Instead of the laid back June she was used to spending time with, now she was locked in a suite with an agitated June who couldn't sit still long. June finished her emails, took another bath, packed most of her things and then returned to the online streams of people's mundane lives and wars around the world.

They were surprised when more knocks were at the door.

"Ms. Cho? It's Patrolman Lewis."

June opened the door leaving the security lock engaged again.

"Sergeant Caldwell asked me to bring you and Ms. Wethers to the security office here to review the video footage from this morning."

"This can't be good." Farrah wasn't in any mood to

change out of her leggings and oversized shirt to be more presentable. She grabbed her phone and the suite's key card. "We better go see what they found. Maybe we'll get lucky."

"I'm drinking at lunch just so you know."

"I would be more surprised if you didn't."

They walked behind their police escort through the long hallways. Farrah felt like everyone they walked passed was staring at them. Of course they were - it was natural to look if a uniform was spotted. The stares felt more judgmental. The eyes were on her and June not only on the cop.

"I appreciate you covering up front legal costs. Jackson said the accounts still can't be accessed, but they should be available soon."

"I told you not to worry about it. Besides, I was the one almost killed. I plan on recouping that expense from either Caressa Lamour or the lodge for not providing the security they promised."

The closet marked "Security" on the door was windowless and already cramped with two people inside. Markos apologized for the tight space and reiterated that the lodge didn't have full-time security personnel. He owned his own consulting business that provided assessments, recommendations, and equipment installations. He wasn't any kind of officer, bodyguard, or rent-a-cop. His clarifications didn't do anything to make the women feel more confident or safer - quite the opposite. He was the type of guy who liked to play pretend cop. Thankfully, they had two genuine ones on the case.

"Thank you for coming. I'd like you take a look at the two feeds where the hooded person who attacked you was visible on cameras."

"Only two?"

Markos didn't even look up at June when he answered her. "They didn't have much of a budget for upgrades when I gave them recommendations. There aren't even cameras on the out-building entrances. Only here in the main lodge, a couple at the pool, and one in each parking area."

"So there's no chance at all that you have footage from Milton's fall?" Farrah hoped to take advantage of the surveillance opportunity, but he said there was nothing. "That's disappointing."

Caldwell pressed himself as far back as possible in the claustrophobic room. He needed to tilt his head to keep from knocking it into a shelf filled with backup tapes. Farrah stood behind Markos and had completely invaded the personal space of Caldwell. June's breasts were practically in Markos' face when she leaned over to see the black and white monitor.

"With so little light in the pool area, there's not much detail." Markos played the pool view a few times and froze the screen at the point where the attacker was closest to the camera mounted above the door when they exited.

"I can't tell anything from that. I guess it's a white guy." June bowed her head in frustration. When she picked it up, Markos changed the display to the other view.

"Here we have a good shot of the hallway. There's full lighting. But this person exits the door, his face is still hidden by the sweatshirt, and then he bolts down the hall away from the camera." Markos replayed that scene a few times and toggled back to the darker, blurry shot of the only time the person was facing a camera in the pool.

Farrah's wiggling around didn't help the issue with Caldwell's lack of space in the corner behind the desk. She tried facing June then facing him. Either way her butt was backed up against his front or they pressed against each other face to face. Awkward no matter how she tried.

Caldwell made his best attempt at dignity. "I've asked Markos to circulate that image to the staff here. We put it on an official form and shared it with the cosmetics people and the local news."

June stood upright leaving Markos to shift nervously from her being so close. "We have nothing in other words?"

"I'm sorry. It's unlikely this will be helpful. Unless you can see something there that's familiar. It's a plain sweatshirt. Not much to distinguish him from anyone else. What about the shoes? They look black. Have you noticed anyone with black sneakers?"

"I haven't noticed. Have you, Farrah?"

"No. More than half of the clients I've worked on don't have any clothes on at all. But I'm not sure those are black, Sergeant. If only this were in color. They're certainly not all black. You can see it's much lighter at the laces. And what's that there?" Farrah pointed to something light, possibly shiny poking out from under the sweatshirt. It was something hanging from his belt loop, but not much of it was visible.

"I can't tell." June breeched Markos' workspace again. "Maybe it's a phone holster. Do people still use those?"

"No. But they're usually black anyway. That looks shiny to me." Farrah leaned forward to encroach on Markos' area from his right side. With Caldwell behind her bent-over body, it looked like the opening scene of an adult movie.

Caldwell cleared his throat. "Like I said, it's very little to go on, but make a list of anyone you see that could be a match and call me."

CHAPTER TWENTY-EIGHT

"I thought we would be allowed to go home." Farrah righted herself to look Caldwell in the eye.

"I can't keep you here, but it would be helpful if you stayed and tried to find who attacked Ms. Cho. I'd also like to go back to your suite…" Caldwell must have realized how that sounded after his crotch was separated from her back side by only fabric. "For questions. I think you'd both be more comfortable there."

Officer Lewis would be with them at all times until shift change. They were given specific instructions. If one of them wanted to leave the room, he would be the escort, but then the other one would be stuck in the room and not allowed to open the door for anyone not on the approved list.

"We'll stay together if we aren't allowed to leave." June told Farrah that the whole idea they could identify the suspect was ludicrous. They had virtually no knowledge of the people there. Farrah echoed her desire to be home, curled up on the couch under her favorite blanket.

Farrah worried about how it must have looked to everyone else seeing the two of them walking down the corridors with two police officers. Before, one cop was enough to alert the gossip hounds and social media timelines. With Caldwell behind them and Lewis leading, Farrah and June looked like women accused of witchcraft being lead to the stakes.

On the way, Farrah spotted Micah Maddox, the IT guy. She thought he left to fight off the hackers from his office. He was at the front desk and handed paper to the desk clerk, Cynthia. She looked down at the letter or whatever it was and looked alarmed, then made a phone call. As Farrah's entourage got closer, she saw Gracie Banks across the lobby headed straight for Micah. Both of them clutched their phones. Farrah realized the only time Micah probably let go of his was during his massage appointment. Tech gurus were practically cyborgs with devices on them at all times. Farrah used hers as a tool to get through life not as life itself.

"Hey, I have an idea." June spoke in a low voice, not that what she wanted to say couldn't be in front of the police, but Farrah appreciated any effort not to draw more attention to them. "There's Gracie. She's their online expert, right?"

"Yeah. Why?"

"She's incredibly popular. I can see why she's in charge of their social media. She has a hundred thousand QuickPic followers on her own account."

"So? Sounds like she's good at her job."

"No, I mean her profiles, not the company's. Anyway, someone with that kind of following is like a celebrity. Let's get her to leave you a good review. You said she seemed to enjoy the massage, right?"

"Right now? While we have bodyguards and people are staring?"

"Yes. Now is the perfect time. She'll see these guys and it'll be intimidating even if it's subliminal. Please! Let me do this!"

"Ask them." Farrah pumped her thumb towards Caldwell at the rear flank.

June spun around and smiled at him. Her saccharine plea to pause for a minute was unnecessary, but amusing to watch. Farrah envied the bravado in June's refusal to sit idly by while Caressa Lamour tried to keep them quiet and could crush Farrah's business with the weight of their bank accounts and lawyers.

"Excuse me. Gracie?"

Micah and Gracie looked at June and Farrah. Just like June predicted, both of them darted glances to the cops fifteen feet away and engaged in their own conversation.

"Micah, hi! I thought you'd left?" Farrah wanted to sound as friendly as possible, but with the stress of their week, she had no idea how to moderate whether her tone was friendly, snarky, or condescending. "It's good to see you back."

"Hi. The hacking is under control, but I have some things to do here before the conference is over."

"What would you have to do from here?" June wasn't going to let something like confidentiality keep her from inquiring about anything. Worst he could say was "no comment." Instead he answered without giving too much away.

"Since our employees have been using the business center, I need to make sure there's no proprietary data on the lodge's computers and scrub them. People were notified not to use them anymore and if they need laptops, I have several they can borrow." He gestured to the dolly next to him.

"Oh, interesting." Farrah wondered why Caressa Lamour hadn't implemented guidelines for computer use before the employees even arrived, but they probably hadn't thought they'd be hacked and under the scrutiny of activists and the press either.

"So, Gracie," June placed her hand on Gracie's shoulder, letting it drift down to her elbow like she was comforting her. "We forgot to mention something after your appointment with Farrah. If you enjoyed your experience, we would absolutely love for you leave a positive review. You too, Micah. Any good review is welcome."

Farrah was grateful that June's thoughts were about her business after the horrible ordeals they went through in just a few days' time. The selflessness and generosity never felt like June wanted something in return. At such a disastrous moment in her own life, she found time to do something nice for Farrah.

"Yeah, sure." Gracie's brow furrowed between her eyes. It was almost the exact same look Farrah's daughter would give to her when they weren't relating on the same level. It was that whatever-you're-crazy-go-away look.

The desk clerk was joined by someone else who looked like she wielded more authority. Micah took his attention off June and resumed his real mission.

"That's no problem. You can use the suite you had and you know where the business center is, right?" The manager handed Micah back the paper he presented before.

"Yeah, thanks." He picked up the shoulder bag that had been at his feet and tipped back the small handtruck loaded with a bin of laptops. "See you later, Gracie. We'll shoot those pix at three, okay?"

"Okay, thanks." Gracie watched him leave, but then her natural instinct was to look down at her phone as she seemed to do every sixty seconds. "It was nice to see you, but I gotta go."

Farrah and June continued the trajectory toward their suite with the two officers behind them. Lewis must have thought there was no threat of anyone accosting them from the front, but more likely he preferred to stick close to Caldwell and have someone to talk to.

June reached for her key card well before they were near their room. "Do you think they're involved?"

"Who?" Farrah looked around to see if June meant someone in the vicinity.

"Micah and Gracie."

"I don't know. She uses computer things and he fixes computer things. It was probably just business."

"I thought I saw something between them. There was a spark there." Finding a menial distraction like being nosy continued to keep June from their obsessing about their problems.

"Who cares? They're two attractive young people. Do young people even date anymore? Do they just hook up? I have no idea what my daughter's generation does."

"Well if you were online more, maybe you'd have a better understanding of the world around you."

"I hate the world around me." Farrah glanced at her phone. No blinking notification. No email icon lit up. She obliterated her schedule for the day, so no appointment reminders buzzed. Maybe she was missing out on a whole part of life. "I use the internet. You make me sound like a caveman."

"Relax. I'm not picking on you, sweetie. I just think you'd realize what's out there. Jackson spends a lot of time online. I probably spend way too much time online, but it's addictive. Maybe if you did, you'd find something that revitalizes you the way building that dog park is doing for him."

"See. You admit you're too addicted to all those social networks. You're not exactly out in the world enjoying it. You're at home watching the world. I don't see why you're any better for it than I am."

"I love you, sweetie, but you can't stand still. Everything and everyone is connected in a matter of a few clicks and taps."

They were only six rooms away from their door. "Let me tell you about clicks and taps: right now, my bank accounts are frozen, my face has been plastered all over the news, there were reporters at my house two days ago. I don't see how being out there and connected with strangers is good."

June swiped the card and pushed the door.

Farrah followed her in. "I half expected to find the place ransacked with our run of luck."

What they did find was the phone blinking and a voicemail from the front desk. Cynthia said she was fully informed of their unique situation and whenever they want housekeeping to tend to their room, call down to her and she'll take care of it.

"We need to talk about why Ms. Cho was targeted. Why not you, Ms. Wethers?" Caldwell took a seat at the table with them while Lewis returned to standing watch outside the door.

"I guess there's no chance of mistaken identity." Farrah ran one hand over the top of her ponytail.

"The absolute only thing I can think of is someone found out I've been snooping through their online profiles. Since one of them is probably Milton's killer, I can see how that would piss someone off." June pulled the laptop over and showed Sergeant Caldwell the type of things she had been doing all week.

"You're not hacking into them, are you? That's a big problem."

"No. No. Nothing like that. I'm surfing around and viewing their profiles on sites that are personal and professional. That's how I saw the resume for Sandra Schaeffer that showed where she once volunteered for an animal shelter. I… we thought it might be a connection between the animal rescue and the BARN organization."

"You have to be registered on that resume site to view anyone else's profile, correct?"

"Yes."

"I'm familiar with that site, Ms. Cho. Maybe you have

your notifications turned off if you aren't actively job hunting. But, I've got some bad news for you."

"What?"

Farrah grew more worried by the second that June got herself into serious trouble by thinking all that clicking and tapping on social media was beneficial.

Caldwell pulled the laptop closer and asked for permission to go to the ProKinect dashboard. "I think it's somewhere over here." He clicked through from where June would edit her work history to the tab with her privacy settings. "Yep. There ya go. You have all these unchecked."

"So?"

"Read this one."

June looked mortified. There was a checkbox next to a setting to turn on or off email notifications for whenever someone else viewed her profile. "What the hell is that? What does that mean?"

"Let me show you." Caldwell took out his phone and opened his work email. "I'm on here to network with other cops around the country that I meet at training seminars and stuff. I don't have too much use for it. But I noticed that when I signed up, my inbox was inundated with junk. They have a million notifications for every little thing on that site including that one I showed you."

He held his phone over so June could read an email he opened. She cradled his hand in both of hers. The look on her face showed how confused and worried she was.

"Chief Brockton viewed your profile. Wait. What? I don't understand." June took the phone right out of his hand and held it out for Farrah to read.

"I don't either. What does that mean?"

"It means that on this professional networking site, you can't just go surfing around. It's for job hunters and employers so when someone's resume is viewed, they know. It sends them an email notification."

"That's insane!"

"Holy shit! See, June! I told you to be careful about that stuff!"

CHAPTER TWENTY-NINE

SERGEANT Caldwell continued to have Patrolman Lewis guard Farrah and June for as long as they were willing to stay at the lodge. He lifted their sequestration in the suite, but they weren't completely off their leashes. They were free to go wherever they wanted as long as it was a place where an officer could shadow them. That meant areas like the women's locker room of the pool building were off limits though neither of them had any desire to return there. For the remainder of their stay, Lewis or another officer would be outside the door.

"Oh god, it's Chloe." Sitting at the table, Farrah was disappointed when she read the screen of her ringing phone. "Uh huh... What... Why... That's fine." Her conversation was stunted at best.

Caldwell stood nearby. His presence did continue to give Farrah a boost to her sense of security which previously had been crippled.

"Everything okay, Ms. Wethers?"

"Fine, I think. That was Chloe Griffin from Caressa Lamour's human resources department."

"Uh huh. I met her on Monday. She was rather upset after Mr. Byron's accident."

Farrah glanced at June. "Accident? You still think Milton tripped and fell off that cliff even after June was attacked?"

"I really can't say."

"Sure." She raised her eyebrows at June expressing silently and mutually that they knew he was full of crap.

"What was that about Ms. Griffin?"

"Oh that was weird. She said Brad Dubray is requesting to meet June and me. I think he probably wants to gauge whether we'll sue them into the next century for not taking safety precautions seriously on their company retreat."

"When do we have to do that?" June sat on the back of the loveseat. Her shoulders began to slump forward again — clear evidence her stamina was shot.

"I don't know. She only wanted to see if we were staying here until Friday like we originally planned. It seems Brad has been going back and forth to the office putting in long hours."

"I guess he's trying to prove his dedication to the board to secure that job." June wasn't going to give him any benefit of the doubt. She let her beliefs known that she saw everyone at

Caressa Lamour as greedy and selfish, looking to step on each other to climb up the ladder or at least hold on for dear life and avoid downsizing.

"I'm surprised too. They're still dealing with the animal rights people and the news media while their CEO has to learn how to do his job." Farrah pulled out a chair around the table and gestured for Caldwell to join her there.

June fidgeted with one of her shoelaces. "I don't think we should meet with Brad without our lawyer present."

"She said he only wanted to meet us not like 'have a meeting' with us."

"Ms. Cho might be right. For your own best interests. You might accidentally say something that comes back to bite you in the ass. Pardon my saying."

Caldwell had almost twenty years of experience dealing with the guilty and innocent. Like most members of law enforcement, his cynicism wasn't well-hidden. Most people were guilty of something to some degree. If the cosmetics company's new CEO wanted to meet, it wasn't going to be to chuckle over a cup of tea while June recited the anecdote of nearly being killed in a pool.

June walked over to a comfortable plush chair and let her body melt into it. "Maybe we should email her back and remind her of our lawyer's contact information. I honestly don't feel like talking to that woman again."

Farrah agreed with June's proposal. Emailing and copying their attorney on the message was the best approach. That way Chloe would see that they weren't messing around or taking any interaction with Caressa Lamour less than seriously.

"Sergeant, before you go, I had one more question." Farrah swiveled her legs under the table and aimed them in his direction. She leaned forward on her elbows when she spoke. "Regarding the security cameras - you and Markos said there weren't very many of them around the premises for whatever budgetary reason…"

"That's correct."

"But I saw the housing for cameras at the front and back entrances."

"Yes. That's where a couple of them are. And like Markos said there's a few around in certain areas like the front desk or anywhere there's money, the swimming pool, and each parking lot. Why do you ask?"

Farrah leaned back. June's curiosity brought her over from the living room area to stand next to them at the table.

"Could you find the footage of Monday morning when Milton Byron left the building? Then we could have a better approximation of when he was attacked. When he died is irrelevant because he died en route to the hospital or shortly thereafter. We need to know when he was pushed off that edge."

Caldwell looked at her and smiled. Something about her had won him over. He wasn't the type of cop to share information outright with persons of interest in connected cases. She and June saw the smile and Farrah returned one in kind.

"Come on now. You know I can't tell you that. There's a pending investigation."

"Why is it pending, Sergeant?" June pulled out the chair closest to her. "You said Milton's death was an accident. So what are you investigating?"

"Are you two a couple of detectives or just busy-bodies?" The smile didn't go away letting them know they were on to something and that he was nearly ready to crack open and spill some information.

"Who us?" Farrah playfully put both hands to her chest and shook her head enough for her ponytail to bounce.

Since Caldwell accidentally admitted there was an investigation surrounding Milton's death and that Farrah and June were more in the position of victims rather than suspects, he was willing to share the smallest detail he knew. He hadn't known these women long, but it was long enough for his seasoned deduction skills to rule them out as assailants.

"You don't go around spreading any rumors or tweeting anything, you got that?"

They shook their heads like a couple of kids waiting to hear about a tale of secret treasure from their grandfather.

"The cameras showed Mr. Byron leaving through the back door right after six in the morning."

Farrah wasn't satisfied without having the chance at follow up questions. "And did they show him returning? He was supposed to have a meeting at eight."

Caldwell looked away from them. He was obviously struggling with how much to say. "No. There was no sign of him coming back into the building."

"You know what that means, right?" June grabbed Farrah's hand.

"That Milton was probably attacked between six and eight because he would have been on his way to have breakfast with Micah and Brad."

Caldwell stood to leave, but Farrah wasn't ready for him to go.

"No. No. Wait. One more thing!"

"You are relentless." He sat back down. "What?"

"Were Brad Dubray and Micah Maddox definitely waiting for him in the small conference room at eight?"

"Yes, they corroborated for each other. And I know what

you're thinking - that doesn't mean they could alibi each other out for the two hours prior. I already figured that out, thank you very much." He tapped the side of his head reminding both of them that he did have a working brain in there.

June looked back at Farrah and recalled the list she made in Farrah's notebook. "So we can't rule out Brad and Micah as having opportunity?"

"No, we can't. I'm not sure if that's good or bad."

"It's bad." Caldwell spoke up a little bit louder with his authoritative voice. "It's bad because you two don't have business poking around in this mess. Ms. Cho, your life is already in danger and we don't know why. For all we know, that culprit could be after the both of you. So just knock it off. Lay low. Enjoy the tranquility of the lake. Then return home to your happy, boring lives without murder. Okay?"

Caldwell clearly hadn't done any research on Farrah or he would have discovered that murder and violent attacks had already appeared in her life not so long ago.

"Look, I'm serious. Keep your noses clean. If Lewis sees you two causing any problems, he's got me on speed dial. Are we clear?"

"Crystal." They said in unison.

Sergeant Caldwell stood for one resolute second and headed for the door. "I'll call you later to make sure everything is all right. And I swear, I will be in constant communication with Officer Lewis so just put these thoughts out of your heads right now."

The ladies walked him to the door to bid farewell and thank him for all of his time and effort. A little schmoozing could keep them in his good graces. Plus, Farrah thought he was an all right guy anyway and wasn't out to cause him any trouble intentionally.

CHAPTER THIRTY

"DO you think that was weird?" Farrah said closing the door behind Sergeant Caldwell. She saw Officer Lewis guarding their suite as promised.

"This entire week has been weird. You'll have to be more specific." June went to the mini fridge for a cold energy drink. She said it was vile and continued to down it anyway.

"I mean about Sergeant Caldwell asking us to stay and try to identify your attacker. He's not forcing us or anything, and it's nice that we can roam about, but still... we did say we wanted to go home." Farrah took the small coffeepot and filled it with tap water. She ran it through the brewer without coffee in order to get some hot water for tea. Unfortunately she wasn't home on her couch enjoying a toasty beverage with her cat in her lap. Instead, she was still stuck at that Lodge of Horrors with a killer on the loose.

"Yeah, I do think it's weird. But he had a good point. All he wants us to do is watch people and make a note of their shoes to jog our own memories. It's not like we're brandishing pistols and making citizens' arrests."

Despite being granted permission to leave the suite, neither woman was particularly excited about doing so except to get lunch. Patrolman Lewis kept his distance while they carried their plastic trays from the dining hall to the seating area around the glowing fireplace.

Farrah carried her messenger bag containing the laptop and the notebook they had been using to brainstorm about suspects.

"Sweetie, you're being way too obvious. Don't crane your neck like you're looking at a car crash on the highway." June's tips on how to spy on already cautious people hadn't convinced Farrah that staying at the lodge was the right thing for them to do.

There were few things that could have distracted Farrah but how delicious the food was one of them. For a resort catering to corporate types, the chefs had an excellent beat on healthier choices that didn't taste like cardboard.

Relaxing was out of the question. Farrah looked down at her phone and saw a new text from her boss asking how things were going. Plus, she and June had separate emails from the attorney they hired for their case. So far, all he had accomplished were small tasks for them like replying to Caressa Lamour on their behalf. June fronted the retainer with her growing credit card balance.

"Tanneson Martin, attorney at law? Which is his first name and which is his last?" Farrah savored the last bite of her sandwich with the final taste of avocado, sprouts, and roasted red pepper.

"I don't care about his name as long as he can do the job. He came highly recommended. He says here," June scrolled through the email on her phone, "that he will accept my retainer and take the job with confidence that I can get them to pay my attorney's fees if we go to court over this."

"So he's thinking a settlement is possible?"

"Sounds like that's the preference and I'm fine with that."

"Do you really think they'd pay anything? Wouldn't that make them look guilty of neglect or endangerment?" Farrah neatly gathered the empty plates and bowls. She stacked their trays together to make more room on the table instead of waiting to flag over a staff member to remove them.

"They don't have to admit they're guilty of anything, but while we're here working for them, they are responsible for our safety to a degree. It's not like I intentionally put myself in harm's way - which is exactly what half those outdoor activities look like! They'll be able to pay because they have the money and insurance. They'll say it's because they feel bad, even though they don't. And they can do all that without admitting guilt. It's a win-win."

"I don't suppose I can walk the dirty dishes back to the dining hall alone?"

June took a gander at Lewis standing tall, looking back and forth through the people that passed. "Probably not. Just leave the tray over there." She pointed to an empty end table between two chairs adding to her idea that the staff should be waiting on them hand over foot anyway.

Farrah looked like a deer caught in headlights when she spotted Derek and Sagari walking from the busy hallway into the seating area. He saw her too. His gaze lingered longer than it needed to. It was clear, he wanted her to see them.

"Has he messaged since you sent him away before?"

"No. Looks like he moved on anyway. Funny, because he said he didn't know Sagari very well and what he did have to say wasn't very nice."

Sagari wore jeans that looked designer because they fit her so perfectly and a white sweater with the collar of a red shirt folded over the neckline. Her black hair was French braided, one of the styles June often wore. It appeared that she noticed that Derek was distracted by something and followed his gaze to see

June and Farrah sitting at a table alone. She didn't wave, but at least directed a smile their way before resuming her focus on him.

"I would like to speak with him before we leave for home. I hate the way he looked at me when I wouldn't let him in the room."

"You were following orders from the police. He'll either get over it or he won't. If he doesn't understand then he's a bigger prick then I thought he was."

"June, please."

"Sorry."

Farrah dug into the messenger bag and set up the laptop. She slid it over to June and made a remark about staying off that professional networking site for good. She kept the notebook for herself and opened to the table they made listing the suspects.

"What are we supposed to do? Sit in high traffic areas and look at people's shoes?" June hesitated before logging into any of the networks.

"I guess so, but we need to be nonchalant about it. He said we could do whatever we wanted and the management said we were welcome to schedule private sessions with their guides or trainers." Farrah wasn't interested in thrill seeking. Any other day, she would have been more curious about what the conference center had to offer in terms of adventurous exercises, but after the crash course in rappelling and then the dangerous attack at the pool, she had enough adrenaline rushes. There had to be something they could do instead of sitting around. Whatever they decided, their police escort would be there which took away some of her worry.

"Do you honestly think this is a real assignment or Caldwell's way of keeping us occupied so we don't get into more trouble?" June avoided the professional resume site and opened the top four networks logging in as herself instead of Farrah's business accounts.

"Probably a little of both. He doesn't want us to leave town because inevitably he'll need to talk to us again." Farrah tried to look anywhere but in Derek's direction. She saw Patrolman Lewis answer his cell phone and she wondered if the days of cops using radios were a thing of the past.

When Lewis ended his call, he approached their table. Unfortunately that caused everyone around to stop what they were doing in order to spy on them. Farrah saw Sandra Schaefer in one of the big comfortable chairs. She held her phone in a way that looked like she was snapping pictures not texting privately nor minding her own business. One more moment of Farrah's life that would end up on the internet out of her control.

"Officer, people are taking our pictures. They're probably sharing that crap with the whole company, the whole world. It doesn't feel any safer here. Can you please recommend to Sergeant Caldwell to let us leave?" Farrah bobbed her head trying to show the cop in which direction she noticed the cell phone activity.

"I'm sorry, ma'am. It's not even his call ultimately. He ran everything by the chief. I came over to let you know that I'll be relieved by another uniformed patrol officer any minute now." Lewis assured them that they were safe and could reach out to Caldwell if they truly felt like their lives were in danger again.

The next officer to babysit them was Neudorff. She looked fresh from the academy which probably meant two things: she was hyper-vigilant and she needed the overtime pay. After Lewis introduced them to Neudorff, she paced the area for a while and eventually stood guard like her predecessor.

Bloop. Bloop. Bloop.

June's chat window kept alerted her to new messages. She didn't show any expression while replying.

"Who are you chatting with?"

"Whitney."

"Are you insane? She's been a primary source of the trouble this week. I don't care how sweet she comes off." Farrah voiced her change in opinion on pretty much everyone that they had dealt with that week. Whitney Gallagher, the heartbroken former intern and whistleblower, was near the top of Farrah's list. She was only beat out for the prestige title of World's Worst Pain in the Ass by Chloe Griffin from HR. She wouldn't admit to June if Derek's name was on her shit list. It was, but she was too embarrassed to say so.

Farrah reached over and closed the laptop on June's fingers. "Now that the police believe Milton was murdered, how do you know that her online activity isn't being monitored by the FBI?"

"How do you know they aren't monitoring us? They probably are, ya know." June pushed Farrah's hands off the computer and reopened it. "And you might be curious to know that Whitney said she never heard anything about Dr. Singer transferring to the Caressa Lamour headquarters in France."

"Shhhh! You're still snooping into Derek and his ex-wife?" Farrah's voice cut out when she got to "Derek" and mouthed his name.

"I think there's something suspicious about it. Whitney happens to be the only person that knows about Caressa Lamour and isn't part of them. I think we could get some good information from her."

"Why isn't she in jail?"

"You said it yourself - she might be considered a whistleblower since she used to work there. But since she's not currently an employee and her job isn't threatened, that could mean she isn't technically a whistleblower. I'm not sure how it works since the company is a French corporation and we're not talking about national security. For now, the only thing she can be convicted of is trespassing or disturbing the peace like the other protesters. Maybe corporate espionage stuff. I'm no lawyer."

Before dinner, they killed some time outside in beautiful wooden rocking chairs on the large wrap around veranda. Farrah handed June her phone in order to upload pictures to the laptop. Officer Neudorff stood out of their way and started to loosen up as the fresh air and view of the lake presented a sense of serenity, false that it may have been.

June put the files in a folder and opened them in a preview window. She clicked through them slowly. "There's a lot of shoes here, but none of them look like we're getting any closer. They start to all look the same."

Farrah agreed. They put the laptop away and tried to enjoy the view before sunset.

CHAPTER THIRTY-ONE

THURSDAY

SERGEANT Caldwell made arrangements for Officer Neudorff to spend the night with Farrah and June. Instead of making her stand, bored out of her skull, in the hallway all night long when no one would likely be passing by, she agreed to sleep on the loveseat. The door had the key card lock and the secondary security mechanism which they routinely used anyway. Neudorff kept her firearm on the end table. She didn't wear actual pajamas. Stretchy athletic wear hugged her muscular body. She even kept sneakers on all night.

Neudorff never got into a heavy sleep. She got up every couple hours to walk around the suite and check outside the door. All was quiet.

"Good morning, um… what do I call you?" Farrah came from her private bedroom stretching her arms overhead and leaning left then right to loosen up.

"Neudorff." She said it like, *what the hell do you think you call me?*

"Got it. Neudorff. We'll probably go for breakfast in the dining hall. They have a good buffet. Are you allowed to eat with us?"

"Yes, ma'am. I have to stay alert though. Ready to jump up and go as soon as need be." Neudorff's stretching shamed Farrah who felt like she was watching a professional trainer on a video. Next thing Farrah knew, Neudorff's face was in the carpet for push-ups. Manly ones too not the sissy girl ones on knees. Full plank. It was impressive.

Farrah was in and out of the shower before June even wandered out of her room. It was their last full day stuck at the retreat center. She put on her go-to cargo pants and layered a couple of shirts as had been her off-duty fashion each day.

When June finally appeared, Neudorff finished up fifty sit-ups and moved on to side planks. "We're not required to do morning calisthenics, are we?"

"No, ma'am."

"Uh huh." June turned away from the cop thinking about how the young woman needed to enjoy her figure as long as it lasted, because eventually her ass will show signs of sitting in a patrol car day after day, night after night.

"Hey, Caldwell and I spoke last night before I fell asleep."

"Why did he call you? I was the one who was attacked."

"I don't know. I guess he felt like I was another bodyguard for you or something. Aren't you more curious about what he said instead of which one of us he said it to?"

"Sure. Go 'head."

Farrah told June that Caldwell would personally be by their side for the next shift at noon so Neudorff could leave and resume her regular duties.

"Could'a told ya that." Neudorff picked up her neatly folded uniform and headed into the bathroom.

"But… you didn't." Farrah didn't mumble until Neudorff was well out of earshot.

As soon as they were all ready, they sat down for breakfast at a table along the back wall of the dining hall. Farrah tried to make the best of the bodyguard situation. Her friendliness with Neudorff was a little inflated, but she thought if they looked like they were just three friends getting together for breakfast in a remote retreat center in the woods, everyone around would ignore them.

"Neudorff, let me ask you something woman to woman and also woman to law enforcement." Farrah fussed with the cantaloupe in her fruit salad. She hated cantaloupe but wanted the apples and scarce blueberries. "I want to text someone that may or may not be a suspect. Yea or Nay?"

She chewed three times and swallowed. Her eyes went from Farrah to June and back. Her pursed lips already had that *are-you-out-of-your-mind?* look which was emphasized even more when one her eyebrows crinkled.

"Are you serious?"

"She's serious. I already told her to keep her distance. But she's caught up in the douchey charisma of Derek Davis because he's hot."

"I think you should listen to your friend here. Someone tried to hurt her and someone else died. Honestly, I'm surprised you haven't run screaming from this place." Neudorff resume chowing down on the yogurt and granola side dish that topped off her huge portion of eggs and potatoes.

"Hey! We wanted to run screaming, but your boss told us to stay put in case he has more questions for us. Not to mention doing his job for him." Farrah kept her tone as sing-songy as possible for her disguise of being friends with the cop. Instead, she came off like an angry bitch.

"I was wondering why you were taking pictures of people's feet. Thought it was a fetish thing."

"Ewwww!" Farrah and June had identical reactions to the thought that they were never going to scrub from their minds.

June filled up her mug from the carafe that a server dropped off earlier. At least the staff got the coffee right by giving most tables a full pot right away even at a buffet.

"What my friend means is that we had the impression we weren't allowed to leave because of Sergeant Caldwell. He said he needed us to stay as if we were persons of interest. I mean, that's absurd. I'm the one that was drowned."

"Nearly drowned." Neudorff didn't mess around with her deadpan corrections in semantics.

"Oh and by the way, you two may be giving me grief about wanting to contact Derek. Did you know that this one here has been instant messaging with a suspect?"

"No, I did not know that. You want to fill me in, Ms. Cho?"

June's glare beamed over her coffee cup as she sipped. "I'm trying to get information, not flirt. There's a huge difference."

Neudorff listened to June's explanation about chatting online with Whitney. Farrah reveled in the lecture that could put June in her place for her hypocritical behavior. Only, it didn't happen.

"That's not the wisest thing, but I agree with you. It's different than flirting."

"Ha! See!"

Farrah choked on a blueberry, but managed to get a few words out. "How could you side with her?"

"You asked. Does Caldwell know you have a romantic relationship with someone here?"

"Um… I don't know. I guess so. Lewis was here when Derek came to the door to see me." The blood rushed to her face, but not solely from the choking. "And wait just a minute. I am not romantically involved with him. Exactly. One could say."

"Neudorff, what do you call when you stay out all night with a stranger?"

"I wouldn't know." Neudorff didn't give off a virginal vibe, but her all-business personality probably meant she didn't date much.

"So you're not into dating… men? Women?"

"Men. And not right now. I was seeing someone when I went into the academy. Another cop. We're better off as friends. Now, enough about my personal life. Tell me more about this guy you're involved with." Neudorff finished her orange juice while waiting for Farrah to answer.

"I would like to hear more about what kind of information Whitney has shared."

"We'll get to that. First, you." She pointed at Farrah. Neudorff had a ways to go on her intimidation techniques. She was getting there, but she still looked a decade too young for Farrah to easily obey.

She cradled the thick coffee mug in her hands. It wasn't even hot. There was barely any coffee left in it. What was left, she didn't want. But she wanted the comfort of holding something and options were limited when sitting around a table in public view with people staring at the uniformed companion to Farrah's right.

She stared at the dregs of coffee and swirled it around. Her shoulders lifted and dropped hard.

"I didn't sleep with him. I didn't even spend the night."

June's shock was not restrained. "What? Why didn't you tell me? Why would let me believe that you cheated on Jackson? Why would you let me worry about you getting involved with him?" She kept going until Farrah was able to interrupt.

"You assumed I had. And I was just as ashamed as if I had. I'm not saying nothing happened. 'Things' happened. But I stopped at a certain point. It's still wrong and I feel like garbage about it."

June and Neudorff were equally engrossed by the revelation. This was not the kind of attention Farrah wanted. She felt like her body could lose all strength, slide under the table, and turn into a puddle of scarlet goo.

"What exactly happened?" June was going to get the steamy details out of Farrah eventually. Asking for them in front of Neudorff was risky.

CHAPTER THIRTY-TWO

FARRAH'S eyes quickly flashed to the cop then back to June. There was no point in going back. She couldn't avoid telling the story now. Neudorff also had a right to know. She rocked back against the chair, couldn't get comfortable, and sat forward again. Still gripping the mug, but she let her elbows support her against the table.

"We were in the solarium where they've been teaching the yoga classes." She stared in the sad, cold cup of coffee as she talked about her brief make-out session with this hot man she had only recently met. "We were practically having sex right there on the planter ledge. I admit it was exciting. People occasionally walked down that hallway and it was like we were about to get caught at any second. I never did anything like that before. Not since I was raging with hormones in college, of course."

"I didn't hear you come back to the room." June didn't even ask if Farrah wanted it, but she took the carafe and filled her coffee cup for her.

"I was as quiet as possible. It was about two in the morning. He asked me to go back to his room. And I said yes. I shouldn't have. I know that. But I did."

"Did he force himself on you?" Neudorff's posture grew more erect. Her left palm flattened against the table's surface. Her right hand crumbled a napkin.

"No. No. I swear. But it was going too far." She paused as much as possible and eventually confessed that they had gotten as far as clothes being off. "He started doing things to me that I haven't had in a very long time. I felt wanted. I felt desired. Maybe it was all the alcohol. I don't know. But I didn't want to stop. It felt too good."

June and Neudorff stared at Farrah's face. Her muscles had softened. Confessing to them let out a lot of her stress. But it wasn't the same as if she had to confess to her husband.

"But you did stop?"

"Yes. It wasn't easy. But reason and responsibility nagged at me until I couldn't ignore them any longer."

Neudorff kept a tight hold on the napkin. Her other hand wrapped around the empty juice glass with nothing to do. "How did he handle it when you stopped him?"

"Uh, well, there was a lot of heavy breathing, but he was fine. He seemed disappointed. He said so anyway. He said a lot of sweet things."

"I bet." June rolled her eyes and twisted her mouth to one side.

Neudorff looked at June. "So you think he's more of a sleazy player type than an assailant?"

"You're asking me? Yes, I find him particularly sleazy. He's been trying to get into her pants since we arrived. And I think it's transparent that once she told him she didn't want to take it further and she shouldn't speak to him anymore, that he moved on before his next breath."

June filled Neudorff in on spotting Derek with Sagari the day before. Farrah barely moved. Her hands were the only things to fidget and her eyes examined the aftermath of breakfast on their table.

"He was sitting at a table with a coworker and your first thought is that he's banging her? Why do you hate this guy so much?" Neudorff was right. June leapt to conclusions like it was a superpower.

Farrah sat and listened to the explanation. June so convincingly made him come off like Vicomte de Valmont, it was plausible to think he showed up with Sagari right at that moment to stick it in Farrah's face or because he was a sociopath with no feelings. June waxed on about men that couldn't be trusted. Neudorff casually nodded once in a while, but kept her opinions to herself. Eventually Farrah had enough of feeling like a foolish middle-aged woman who was duped by a handsome stranger.

"Stop it. Derek may be a jackass. He may have used me. But one thing he isn't, is a good suspect in Milton's death or in the attack on you. What possible motive would he have?"

"First of all, he kept talking about that China deal he lost. If the executives and the board were firing people through layoffs and because of performance, you know damn well, his name was on a list in red font. It's only a matter of time before he gets canned. Second of all, if he's the type of person who goes after married women, or any women in his field of vision like they're some kind of prey, I don't think it's out of the realm of possibilities that he would want me out of the way since I am with you all the time. He knows I hate him. He knows I don't want him near you."

All the neighboring eyes were no longer on the uniform standing out in the crowd. Farrah was mortified and wanted to hide forever. Her shoulders remained forward and her head bowed, but she spoke up enough for her companions to hear.

"Whitney is part of an eco-terrorist organization. She was sleeping with the man who became the new CEO until her internship ended. And she's practically stalking him." Farrah spelled out the basics for Neudorff's benefit. "Derek didn't benefit from any of this."

Neudorff watched them sitting silently after they got their aggravation out. She told them that they each had valid points, but that their speculation was worthless. What matters was what the police could prove and whether the guilty party faced justice.

"Okay, so how do we do that? How do we figure out who attacked June and get evidence?"

"I shouldn't contradict my superior." Neudorff raised one eyebrow. "If he wants you to stay here and try to find someone you recognize, I'll help until my shift change. Let's go back to the room where it's quiet."

"Shouldn't we be where the people are? To see who fits the build and sneaker fashion of the person on the tape?" Farrah tidied up all the plates and mugs, stacking everything together.

"Not for this."

They walked in line most of the way back to the suite, Neudorff only took a step back when other people cramped the space.

On their way, Farrah saw Micah and Gracie with a box of stuff exiting out the back door. "I wonder what they're up to."

June told her it was unlikely anything sinister. They probably needed samples of the products and other props that

Gracie needed for QuickPic and Corxboards.

Neudorff told June to get comfortable reclining on the loveseat. She propped a pillow under June's knees and another under her head to make her more comfortable. Then asked Farrah to dim the lights.

June hadn't noticed the roughness of the furniture's plaid cushions before. It was the kind of fabric that could take a beating and probably had from years of families with rambunctious kids or drunken salesmen away from their desks for a week.

"I've heard this is a technique therapists use to help people remember things they don't even realize they remember." Neudorff asked June to close her eyes. She counted down from ten and reminded her that they were in a safe space. She asked June to think back to when she was swimming.

"Farrah's phone rang. She got out to answer it and walked into the locker room."

"Good. What then?"

"I swam over to the shallow end to the corner and rested."

"What did you see?"

"Nothing. I closed my eyes."

"What do you hear?"

"There's a hum from the filter. I can hear that Farrah is talking, but it's faint and I don't know what she's saying. Then I can't hear her anymore."

"What do you smell?"

"Chlorine. And humidity. That's weird but I smell the temperature."

"That's good. You're doing fine. You're safe. Keep thinking about the last moment before you felt the hands on you." Neudorff continued to guide June in her memory. She pressed her about her olfactory memory more.

"I smell dirt. And Farrah's bathroom."

"Okay. What do you notice that reminds you of Farrah's bathroom?" Neudorff looked at Farrah and shrugged her shoulders. She couldn't figure out if June shifted to a different memory or if she needed the memory of Farrah's bathroom decoded.

"That's what I smell. Chlorine. Earth. Farrah's bathroom."

The scariest part was when Neudorff guided June through the actual attack. June choked and sputtered. She grabbed at the back of her head because she had slipped and cracked it against the edge of the pool. The memory made it throb again in real life.

"You're safe and fine, June. You have air. You can breathe." Neudorff put a hand on June's shoulder to give the slightest sense of being grounded in reality.

Nothing else new came from the memories. The attacker hadn't spoken to her so there was no voice to think about.

"I'm under the water. I can't see who it is. It's a blurry, dark figure in a hood."

They waited for her to continue on her own. She moved her head side to side against the throw pillow. One hand stayed on the back of her head. The other floated in the air, reaching out for something that wasn't there.

"I see something shiny, but I can't reach it. I can't tell what it is. I hear something. A voice. I think it's Farrah. It's all dark. I don't see anything. Wait. I look around and see the person going out the door, but I still can't tell who it is."

Neudorff emphasized that she was doing fine, but it was time to come back to the room and to reality.

"I use guided meditation pretty often with my clients, but I never even thought to use it for June's memory." Farrah fetched a cold bottle of water from the mini-fridge, cracked the cap open, and handed it to June. "I approve of your unconventional interrogation methods, Neudorff. It's much better than what I've experienced before."

"Better for you to watch, maybe, but that wasn't easy for me to revisit."

"I'm sorry, babe. I know." Farrah put her arm around June and rubbed her back.

"Now we have a little bit more to go on." Neudorff leaned forward and patted June's knee.

"What more do we have? That the person smells like a bathroom?"

"Not just any bathroom," Neudorff said. "Farrah's bathroom. What makes that bathroom different than any other that you thought of it?"

They sat in their triangle wondering about the answer to that question.

CHAPTER THIRTY-THREE

NEUDORFF'S phone rang when they left the room. Sergeant Caldwell was checking in to see if there were any new developments and to remind her that he'd be there at noon to relieve her.

June took a gulp from her water bottle as the three of them walked down the back stairs of the lodge facing the lake.

"Thanks for agreeing to take a walk. I wasn't in the mood to stay cooped up again."

"What should we do? My body is pretty much over all the physical activity I've put it through this week." Farrah slid her sunglasses up the bridge of her nose and scanned the area looking for inspiration.

They agreed to take it easy and walk the grounds to see what was going on. The Caressa Lamour teams were out and about doing their activities. One group headed in the direction Farrah previously walked with Derek to the log balancing challenges. Another group, crossed the dying grass and went over to the tall tree at the edge of the cliff.

"Oh my god. Look at that. Forrest is going to make them rappel and climb?" Farrah pointed out to Neudorff that that was the location of the murder scene. "I can't believe they haven't closed that down for good."

Neudorff mentally counted seven participants and two instructors. "I guess they don't need to cordon it off for the investigation."

June agreed it seemed unwise and insensitive. "I can't believe anyone signed up to spend time there. They all know what happened. Most everyone from the company was out here during the rescue and evac. But there they are — lined up and waiting to risk injury."

They continued getting closer to the rock climbing team rather than head towards the trail through the woods.

Farrah took out her phone and took a few pictures from the distance. "Look who's in that group?"

"Who?" Neudorff still wasn't sure who most people were.

June squinted through her sunglasses. "Is that Brad Dubray?"

"Yes, it is." Farrah couldn't believe it. He returned to the place where his predecessor died. "Pretty damn tasteless, if you ask me."

"Some people play as hard as they work."

Farrah didn't know if Neudorff was talking about herself or making a general observation.

It wasn't only the morbid curiosity compelling Farrah to lead the group over to the rock climbers. She also felt an obligation to the man whose last few minutes were spent with her and the rescue medics.

November was almost as windy as October's hurricane season. The air was filled with the fragrance of the cedars and that distinguished smell of the cold winter approaching.

"Are you interested in joining the lesson?" Forrest recognized Farrah and June, but the uniform caught him off guard.

"Nope. We're merely observing. You don't mind, do you?" Farrah had a feeling she could play the hero card if she needed.

"Not at all. You've already had your crash course." He smiled, keeping up his image of dutiful, fun instructor for the group of cubicle-dwellers.

They watched and listened while Forrest and his assistant helped people get strapped into their harnesses. Rope basics were covered. Helmets were secured. One by one, they teetered over the side and bounced against the rock wall on their way down.

"You sure you don't want to go down under better conditions?"

"I'm sure. Though it does look a lot less terrifying when there's no emergency." Farrah knew that if the circumstances had been different, June probably would be interested in learning how to rappel and climb. It was the sort of thing both of them would be willing to do once to say they had and then never do again. Farrah had her one experience and was quite done.

Forrest was the last one to go down. He looked up at them and waved. Since no one told them they couldn't, Farrah and June continued to take a bunch of pictures. Absolutely none of them were intended for social media.

"Did you notice their shoes?" June's neck was stretched as she looked over the edge. "Several of them are different than your average sneaker. They even look like the same brand."

"Interesting. That's not what caught my eye."

"Wow, you two really are a couple of detectives." Neudorff looked over Farrah's shoulder while she swiped the screen to preview the shots she took.

Farrah stopped on a shot of Brad. His legs were straight. He was angled over the emptiness below, tethered by the rope. His head was turned to look down in the final moment questioning his decision. Farrah pinched and zoomed to his waistline.

"You perv," June said.

"Stop. I'm not looking at that. I'm looking at this." Her finger pressed the image and slid it to bring a certain detail to the center. She zoomed again.

"His carabiner?" Neudorff seemed familiar with the gear. Farrah assumed she was either the outdoorsy type or learned it in the military before her police training.

Farrah pointed to it. It was silver and shiny. Between the unusual Velcro straps on a grown man's shoes and the glint from the carabiner, the ladies knew they were on to something useful in narrowing down their suspect pool. They didn't want to draw attention to themselves so they backed away and walked to one of the well-kept garden areas.

CHAPTER THIRTY-FOUR

INSIDE the dead hedges, they found Gracie posing for pictures on a bench in the middle of the decorative circular sidewalk. Micah was using semi-professional photography equipment - a relatively small DSLR camera with flash and flexible reflector. Behind him were boxes of products, hair and makeup supplies, and another box of clothes, wigs and accessories for Gracie to change her look. The grotto was probably private enough for a pro like her to change clothes without peeping eyes or unauthorized cameras.

"Oh! So sorry to interrupt." Farrah held up her hand to wave while walking through the nearly secret entrance of the trellis covered in dead morning glory vines that the staff neglected to clear away. She should have been looking down because she never saw the misplaced rock in her way which caused her to stumble.

"Ow!"

June tried to reach for her, but Farrah's fall was too quick. She crashed down hard on her knees and hands.

June took Farrah's hand and helped her back to her feet. "Come on. I gotcha."

Farrah thanked her, brushed off her knees and glared at her favorite pants now degraded with a hole.

Neudorff didn't deem Micah and Gracie as a threat though she was interested to know why they weren't participating in anything on the official schedule.

Gracie played with her hair which didn't need to be fixed. She eyed Neudorff's unflattering and unfashionable uniform. "Because of all the bad publicity, my bosses want me to go into overdrive reclaiming our sophisticated and sexy brand identity."

"So we've have to take a ton of photos with Gracie modeling since we're stuck here and don't have her staff of beauty bloggers to carry some of the workload."

June casually opened up the app on her phone and filtered for the #CaressaLamour trends. "Wouldn't the beauty bloggers use their own phones wherever they are to post about the products?"

Gracie practically snorted from the ignorance of the sad, middle-aged discount store shoppers in her presence. "They post from anywhere, but everything is carefully curated. They have some leeway, but I have to approve any posts that the company is going to pay for."

"I know we're interrupting you, but I was wondering something. Do you mind?" Farrah took a seat next to Gracie on the bench before she got her answer.

Gracie put down the Caressa Lamour compact of pale cream foundation that she was pretending to apply for the photos. "I guess we can spare a minute, but we're trying to work with this diminishing sunlight."

Neudorff stayed by the garden's secret entrance. June circled closer to stand next to Micah. Farrah had no idea if her partners planned that, but they made it so neither Micah nor Gracie could make a run for it if they didn't like Farrah's questions.

"Micah, you were supposed to have a meeting with Milton Byron on Monday morning. Is that right?" Farrah looked up at him as he retracted the camera lens making a whirring sound.

"Yeah. With Brad. So?"

"Remind me, what time was that meeting supposed to be?"

"Eight in the morning before the official schedule began. Why?"

Gracie put the compact into the box at her feet and stood up tall next to Micah. "If you're interrogating him about Mr. Byron, you can't. Not without the company's lawyers. We got a memo."

Neudorff tried to stifle the snort when she chuckled about the memo. If that girl was scared of a company memo, she'd cripple in fear at the things Neudorff herself went through in Tehran. Lawyers didn't scare her. They scared Farrah though and the twitch of her shoulder gave out a subtle signal at the mere mention of them.

"Oh, this isn't an official interrogation. Officer Neudorff is here as June's bodyguard. You may have heard that someone here tried to drown her. We're simply trying to get to the bottom of these unfortunate events. You can understand that, can't you?"

Micah didn't return Gracie's desperate gaze. He turned his head to June. "I'm sorry. I heard a rumor, but didn't think it was true."

"Thank you. I'm fine now. But the two of us have felt unsafe from the moment we arrived."

Farrah stayed seated to counterbalance Neudorff's intimidating stature. The bench was terribly uncomfortable. Its sole purpose was obviously for visual aesthetics and not meant to be practical which was a shame, because it seemed like the type of nook where guests or staff could find serenity. After a cursory glance at June, Farrah focused back on Micah.

"Did Milton show up to the meeting at eight?"

"No. I told that detective or sergeant, whatever he was, already. I was there in the small conference room a minute before eight. I started eating while I was waiting. Brad eventually showed up around ten after. Milton never did so we left."

"What time did you actually leave?"

"It was 8:30. I mean, the guy was the boss. We waited longer than we normally would have."

Farrah stood and reached out to shake Micah's hand. He let the camera hang on the strap around his neck and returned the gesture.

"Oh, one more thing," Farrah said. "Where were you before eight? Say from six to eight?"

"In my room."

"He was with me! All. Night." Gracie stood as close to him as possible. He looked uncomfortable at her brazen outburst.

"Oh, okay. So sorry to trouble both of you. We'll let you get back to work." Farrah pushed passed Gracie who stood so firmly planted that she made Farrah brush against her. When she got near the trellis, she looked back. "Thank you for the extra information. Speaking for June and myself, we deeply appreciate a conversation that isn't through lawyers. We aren't interested in finding any more trouble."

CHAPTER THIRTY-FIVE

NEUDORFF waited near the trellis until June and Farrah exited the little sanctuary. She gave one last long expressionless stare to Micah and Gracie. She pivoted and started on her way behind the other two.

"You didn't ask specifically if he went from his room to the conference room."

Farrah wasn't putting any thought into the direction she walked.

"He was much less anxious than when I met him for his massage. That's for sure. He must get a lot of confidence being adored by Gracie in front of people."

They ended up back at the rappelling cliff. The team they watched before was at the bottom where Milton had fallen. Forrest was giving them directions on how to climb up now that they had successfully descended.

"Neudorff is right. We don't know that he went directly to the meeting," June said. "It's a matter of whether or not you believe him."

"Well don't you?"

"I guess so, but I can't tell anymore. All these people seem like they're up to something." June lifted her sunglasses to peer down the edge and scope out the climbers.

"Your paranoia is understandable after a traumatic event." Neudorff moved closer to June. Her hands were free from holding onto her belt as she habitually did. She was alert in case June's balance suddenly left her.

"What do you think, Neudorff? You must have an idea whether Micah was lying about where he was when Milton was right here getting pushed or thrown to his death." Farrah had quite enough of that particular spot and had no interest in peering over the side the way June did.

Neudorff didn't answer until June was perfectly upright and as safe as possible without a tether. "I believe him. Never got the sense he was lying. I think you're right about his behavior with the girl though. He looked confident to me when he answered questions, but when we first walked into their secret garden, he was startled and alert."

Farrah said, "She's beautiful and popular. That's the reason she even has her job. Was he startled by us or was he embarrassed to be caught with her?"

June shook her head. "Just because she's hot doesn't mean she wouldn't embarrass him. Maybe she's the histrionic type."

Farrah wasn't sure where her brain wanted to go with Micah's opportunity to meet Milton alone at the cliff. He didn't seem to have much motive to physically assault him no less murder him. Mentally, she crossed him off her suspect list. She planned to revisit it with June later. She pulled herself from the train of thought when she noticed Neudorff looking in every direction.

"What's wrong?"

"There's something that seems off to me. This part of the grounds is almost completely exposed except for those couple of big trees."

"And what does that tell you?"

Neudorff pointed to the lodge's rear side. "Even if it was so early that a person would think nobody was around here outside in the early daylight hours, how could they be so assured to think that no one would be looking out any of those windows? Most of the back of the building is glass. The staff had to be up and busy getting ready for the first day of the retreat."

"It was risky. That's for sure." June said.

"Not only risky. It almost seems stupid. Careless, even. I'm thinking that no one smart enough to plan a murder would plan it for this spot."

"What if it wasn't planned? What if it was either an accident or something that happened in the heat of an argument?" Farrah's mind raced through the other names on their list: Brad Dubray, Whitney Gallagher and the activists, and Sagari Palla who was terrified about losing her job. Then there was one name that popped into her head last and only because of June's insistence that no one could be ruled out completely: Derek Davis.

"It's entirely possible someone could get away with murder simply because no one saw it happen." Neudorff admitted she wasn't experienced in solving homicides. This would be her first. Her days and nights were spent on patrol catching speeders and past due inspection stickers, drunks, some drug users or sellers, and mostly the small town domestic disturbance calls no one likes to talk about. The only manslaughter she heard of since taking the job was vehicular due to DUI. "This is the perfect kind of scene where it looks like an accident. The owners of this place should have put up some railing and posted warning signs long before. I'm honestly surprised no one cracked their skull sooner."

The first three climbers, all men, were close to the top. Two were working together and courteously helping each other out. The other was Brad, independently and rather expertly making his way. Farrah watched as Brad beat them.

"Why do people find this fun?" Farrah asked.

"It's the adrenaline of completing a challenge." Neudorff sounded like she was talking from experience. What Farrah appreciated was that she wasn't condescending about it. Purely matter of fact.

Brad congratulated the other climbers and posed for a selfie with them. He spent a few seconds tapping on his phone to upload it. He unfastened and removed his helmet. Farrah got nervous seeing him head her way.

"Ladies, hello. Don't you look lovely today?" Brad apparently couldn't be more respectful of a woman in uniform strapped with a Glock. "I hope you got my messages about wanting to meet you this afternoon."

June started out baffled and muttered nonsensical sounds nearly speechless. Unlike what they told Micah and Gracie, there were certain conversations she preferred to have with lawyers present. Talking to Brad was definitely one that made the hair on the back of her neck stand up and goosebumps prickle through her arms.

Eventually, she found words. "Uh, yes. Chloe reached out to us. I believe we set up something for four o'clock."

Brad looped his thumbs through the nylon harness around his pelvis. Farrah caught herself looking because his hands drew attention to his crotch. Maybe he didn't notice where her gaze landed or maybe he knew exactly what he was doing.

"I'm done with my climb if you have a few minutes now."

Farrah turned her head back to view the climbers then back to him, looking in his eyes properly. "Don't you need to help the others? Isn't that supposed to be about supporting your peers?"

He looked back at them then back to Farrah with a devilish smile. "They're fine. I train people to be hard workers and goal oriented."

"As opposed to Milton who emphasized teamwork?" June said.

"Not at all. There's a time for teamwork and a time to take the bull by the horns and do something yourself. Daddy can't always bail ya out, if you know what I mean."

His smile didn't work on June. "I'm sorry, Mr. Dubray, but as I told Chloe and my partner here, I don't think we should be talking to you without the lawyers. I'm just not sure what you could say that isn't about any litigation I may present."

"You're a smart woman, Ms. Cho. And I respect that. So, will your lawyer be here at four?"

"Well, no. The meeting was short notice. There's no way…"

"Say no more. I guess we'll be in touch. Nice meeting you anyway." He shook hands with June and Farrah but not with the officer whose name he didn't seem to want.

Before he bolted, Farrah tried to make amends. "Now wait a minute. June, he only wants to see how you're doing. Isn't that right, Mr. Dubray?"

"Absolutely. I heard what happened and I was appalled. It's unacceptable. And I'm glad to see you're all right." He laid a flat hand across his heart which still wasn't enough to convince Farrah that he was sincere or gave a crap about them, but she wanted information.

Farrah lead him by the arm further away from the pack of Caressa Lamour employees. "We were wondering something and it seems best to me to go to the source rather than get entwined in rumors and gossip."

"Ask whatever you like." He repositioned Farrah's hold on his arm so that he was guiding her. It was a slick move to maintain his dominance.

When they got another twenty feet or so away from the dangerous ledge, Farrah stopped. "Where were you on Monday morning between six and eight?"

Maintaining his smile looked more difficult for him than he was used to. He looked over at Neudorff who stayed close to June since she was the one considered the possible target. His head tilted when his gaze caught the dark-haired, slender woman with the brash attitude. Then he turned back to Farrah. "This does sound like lawyer talk now, Ms. Wethers. I feel like I'm on a witness stand all of a sudden."

"Can you answer the question? As soon as you do, we'll leave you alone to return to your work." She flicked her hand in the direction of the climbers, but it was the smirk on her face that registered in his mind. She may have mocked the seriousness of adults rock climbing for work, but only to gauge his reaction.

Brad crossed his arms over his chest which already looked buff through the tight, bright blue athletic shirt that matched his eyes. "Like I told the police, I was in my room getting ready for my day and headed directly over to the conference room where I met Micah Maddox from our IT department."

"Were you alone in your room? If you don't mind my asking." Farrah tried to be coy and adorable. She doubted it worked.

"Yes. I was alone. I'm not seeing anybody if that's what you're trying to find out." He winked and gave her a pat on the arm. "You have yourself a great day now."

With that, he left and returned to the herd he had abandoned.

CHAPTER THIRTY-SIX

FARRAH and June reclaimed comfortable chairs on the veranda while Neudorff leaned against the railing. The tranquility of the lake was a harsh contrast to the impatience of wanting to leave the lodge and go home.

"Sweetie, I'm glad you got Brad's alibi for Monday morning, but there's still a question about Wednesday morning. Everyone had the opportunity to follow us to the pool." June pulled out her phone and typed notes about her attack and Milton's murder into a notes app. In her notes, there was only person with even a remote grudge against her who was present and that was Derek.

Farrah agreed that she missed out on the only chance to ask Brad more questions. She knew June's logic was sound in wanting lawyers present, but it meant dealing with a lot of other people's schedules. As long as one of the cops was nearby, Farrah felt fine about talking to people.

Neudorff's phone rang. It was Caldwell saying he was on his way. They'd have an hour to overlap before Neudorff could leave. She told them that he wanted to spend some time meeting with the staff and Markos again.

"You're typing a lot." Farrah noticed June's thumbs clicking then pausing then clicking again.

"It's Whitney. She still thinks I have some kind of clout here and can let her back on to the grounds."

"That's the whistleblower, right?" Neudorff took off her sunglasses and hung them from her breast pocket.

June held onto the phone, but let her hands flop to her lap. "Yes. She's still in love with Brad, but you heard him with Farrah. He said he's not seeing anyone. He's over her."

"If he ever had real feelings at all." Farrah's bitterness of her own affair clouded her sentiment.

"Ya know what? She hasn't talked to me. She gave statements to the other officers, but maybe we should ask her to come by. Let's see if she changes her story."

"Don't you have to follow protocol or something? Go through Caldwell?" June looked slightly hopeful.

Neudorff said she was willing to overstep a little if it meant getting a clearer picture. She wasn't a detective, so she could piss off her superior. On the other hand, she was still an officer with authority and there were still two open cases in front of her.

With the cop's blessing, June wrote back to Whitney and asked her to meet with them at the luncheonette a mile from the lodge. It wouldn't give Whitney what she wanted which was to see Brad, but it would give them a chance to ask her more questions.

Sunrise Dairy Treats had walls covered in nostalgia. Old photos showed what it used to be like as a seasonal hut that served eggs and toast for breakfast and burgers with milkshakes at lunch. Next to it was a vending machine for live bait and another for soda. There wasn't more than a counter, the grill, an icebox and a roof big enough to cover the cook who was also the owner Wallace D. Thurman.

Fifty years and several owners later, the Sunrise was a fully enclosed diner opened all year round though they still closed down for two weeks in the winter. They would reopen for the locals that skated when the ice was thick enough; and of course, the fishermen were always out even if that meant cutting through the frosty layer.

The limited greasy spoon menu wasn't exactly vegetarian friendly. Farrah ordered a basket of fries. June and Neudorff ordered coffee and pie. At their booth, June faced the entrance with Neudorff next to the aisle in case anyone approached them in a threatening manner. She ate her slice of cherry pie in five bites and pushed the plate to the end for the waitress to retrieve.

Whitney showed up in a hooded sweatshirt that proclaimed her stance against the bear hunt, a controversial issue in New Jersey. Farrah was relieved it wasn't an official BARN shirt, preferring to keep as much distance as possible from that organization. The last thing she needed was if someone caught her lunching with a radical activist from BARN and then splattered that image all over the internet.

Neudorff stood as their guest approached the booth. Farrah slid across the pale aqua vinyl bench to give her a seat.

"Thank you for the invitation." Whitney grabbed her messenger bag by the thick strap and pulled it over her head to wedge it between herself and Farrah.

It surprised the rest of them to learn that Neudorff hadn't read any of the statements given in the cases. Her involvement as their guard never presented the opening for her to get a look at any of the documentation.

"Just so we're all clear, this is not an official meeting of the police department. I'm not taking your statements. Hell, I won't even ask the questions. June asked if it was all right to meet with you, Ms. Gallagher, and I agreed if both of them stayed together so I could protect them."

Whitney said she understood, but that she wasn't expecting an interrogation. She didn't have any more friends inside Caressa Lamour. June's empathetic ear gave her the only comfort that close to the situation that she had ever received.

"I'm sorry. All I wanted was to talk to someone and you were there. You listened to me." Whitney told the waitress she only wanted a Coke which she drank nervously to do something instead of talking so much.

"Look, Whitney, I'm glad you felt comfortable with me, but I don't think it's in our best interest to be social with you. It's because you leaked the video to BARN and we've been working for Caressa Lamour. Do you see how that puts us, especially Farrah, in a troubling position?"

June's words sent the young woman into a downward spiral. Whitney covered her face with her hands while she suddenly cried. Farrah, always the caregiver, offered her napkins to blow her nose and wipe her face.

"This was stupid. I'm sorry. I should go." Whitney stood up, but when she reached for her bag, Farrah grabbed her by the arm and begged her sit a while longer until she calmed down enough to drive.

"I loved Brad! I still do! I can't think of anything else. I got more involved with the group to try and take my mind off the break up, but the only reason I was with them in the first place was because of the job! And now when I think of the job, I think of him. It's a never ending cycle!"

Farrah took a shot at explaining how everyone goes through heart aches and historically, break ups suck ass. Nothing seemed to help, but Whitney eventually stopped crying. She was distraught and disturbingly desperate.

Neudorff noticed. She glanced up at Farrah then looked down while texting under the table.

The waitress saw the crying young woman and delivered a piece of pie - on the house. Whitney said thank you and stared at it. It was a little too cold for the ice cream that sat on the side of the pastry. Her shaking fingers unrolled the stainless steel utensils that were wrapped up in a paper napkin. She held the fork in her fist with the tongs shooting up towards the stucco ceiling.

Farrah kept watching Whitney, but she fought the instinct to put an arm around her like she would have done to June without a moment's hesitation. The perplex situation prevented Farrah from feeling her phone vibrate in her pocket.

"I only want to congratulate him on his promotion. Honest. He's the CEO now. He could hire me back and that bitch Chloe wouldn't be able to blacklist me!"

"Try the pie, dear. I know junk food always makes me feel better." Farrah's vocal delivery got lower and weaker when she got to the part where she admitted the sugar rushes were only temporary euphoria.

"So you hate Chloe too? There seems to be a lot of that at Caressa Lamour." June didn't look relieved at the confirmation that even insiders hated Chloe. She and Farrah were definitely not fans of hers.

Farrah looked at Neudorff who was fidgeting while keeping her eyes exclusively on Whitney. Farrah thought her cop companion resembled her cat Miles who skulked through the living room towards the front window whenever a strange dog walked in front of their house.

June continued to speculate out loud about the hatred employees had to feel toward the HR department during an era of layoffs and reorganization. "It makes me wonder why she wasn't pushed off the cliff instead of Milton Byron."

"Because I wanted Brad to be CEO and Milton was stupid enough to meet me out there!"

Whitney had everyone's attention including everyone else in the diner.

"Chloe isn't that important! She isn't on the board. No. No! It was Milton who had to go! Milton who turned a blind eye to the animal testing! Milton who wouldn't give Brad any credit for the things he did!"

Whitney's fist shook the fork. Realization of her confession hit her when Neudorff got to her feet. Whitney tried to turn and run for the exit, but Sergeant Caldwell was already coming in the door. She slid a few inches trying to brake and redirect her retreat. It was no use.

The rapidly clicking sound of Neudorff's taser caused everyone to freeze like statues. Whitney's back arched, her arms jerked, then she face planted on the black and white linoleum tiles.

"What the hell just happened?" Farrah was too afraid that guns were about to fire. Despite the overflowing curiosity that wanted her to get up and watch Neudorff and Caldwell tackle Whitney, fear made her curl up into a ball and duck behind the protection of the booth.

June also took cover, but she was lying on her side so she could watch the tackle from under the table. As soon as Neudorff removed the taser and cuffed Whitney behind her back, June maneuvered around the table to hug Farrah.

"She's cuffed. It's okay... We're okay. They have her."

Farrah held on to June, but looked over her shoulder through the glass of the booth's high back. "Still think she's just an over-emotional girl with a broken heart?"

CHAPTER THIRTY-SEVEN

NEUDORFF took Whitney into custody and loaded her into the back of her patrol car. Sergeant Caldwell stayed behind with Farrah and June at the diner before offering to drive them back to the resort.

"Did she really try to attack us with a fork?" Farrah held June's hand in the backseat of the cruiser. She needed the conversation even for one mile to avoid getting familiar with the view from the back of a police car. Even an unmarked one drew stares from everyone around.

June leaned forward to talk through the Plexiglas. "I don't know what she was doing, but she definitely alluded to the fact that she pushed Milton to his death. Hey, Sarge, are we allowed to leave now? I really want to get as far from here as possible."

"I have your statements, Ms. Cho, but I want to sit with both of you to go over everything one last time. We can do it at the lodge or you can come to headquarters. Up to you." He turned the car onto the long gravel driveway to the retreat center. The light of day didn't absolve its creepiness now that it's genuinely a scene of violence.

They walked through the front door and lobby, ignoring every person there. Farrah wasn't sure if people were really whispering new gossip as they walked by or if it was her imagination. It felt real. It was as if all their eyes could beam thoughts into her brain and implant the most outlandish suggestions. *We hate you. We'll find a reason to put you out of business. We blame you for Milton's death. Someone here is still after June.*

The realization of that last imaginary crack made her hackles twitch. She waited until they were securely out of earshot before asking Caldwell what he thought of Whitney's motives and actions.

"Sergeant, after seeing Whitney and her irrational grip on Brad, I understand she thought she had a reason to get rid of Mr. Byron. What I can't piece together is why she would want to attack June? She even said it back there at the table that June consoled her when no one else would."

"That is true. She seemed affectionate towards me which now I look back on and see was rather stalkerish. I just felt so bad for her. I remember what being young and in love and then heartbroken felt like." June tossed her handbag onto the loveseat and joined Farrah and Caldwell at the table.

"What I'm wondering," Farrah looked down at her restless fingers, "is if someone else is still here and sees June as a target. And trust me, I don't know why anyone would. They know she's been my administrative assistant while here, but honestly, they don't know anything about us." Her brows furrowed when she looked up at Caldwell. The corners of her mouth turned down. She wasn't ready to smile and celebrate yet.

Caldwell wasn't convinced danger still lurked. He told them that they were safe and it was normal for them to be hypervigilant after all that they went through. He made some notes in a small spiral notebook, closed it and tucked it into a pocket with his cheap blue ballpoint pen.

"Given the circumstances of Ms. Gallagher's arrest, it seems to me that she's unstable, unhinged. Maybe you weren't reciprocating her friendship enough for her and that set her off to seek revenge. Or maybe she was furious because you wouldn't help her sneak back onto the property. I'm sorry for what you've been through, Ms. Cho, but I don't see any reason to keep a security detail on you."

"Can we leave?" June hadn't gotten a direct answer out of him up to this point. Frustration forced the words through her teeth clenched in her locked jaw.

"Yes, ma'am. You can leave. I have your information. I'm sure we'll need to call on you regarding the assault charges during due process." He stood and buttoned his sports coat.

"Attempted murder, you mean." June didn't hold back. Luckily, she didn't alienate Caldwell. She needed him to sway the prosecutor on which charges could possibly stick.

Caldwell thanked them for their time. They returned the gratitude in kind since he had provided protection and then showed up in the nick of time to arrest Whitney. Farrah and June later discussed how Neudorff had everything under control, but it was additional relief to have him there.

"She's pretty badass. I'm gonna miss having her around." June moved her bags closer to the door eager to leave, but Farrah was still gathering all her luggage.

Farrah agreed that Neudorff ended up being a cooler companion than she originally assessed. "I need to call the front desk to ask them to have that maintenance guy help us with all the equipment again."

"I'm starving." Either the stress was letting up inside June's tense body or nothing could get in the way of her wanting food. She pulled her wallet out of her handbag and looked to see how much cash she had on her.

"Me too." Farrah took a seat at the table again. She held her phone.

"Spill it." June broke Farrah's odd concentration at the screen she hadn't even turned on.

"Huh? What? I'm just thinking."

"You're thinking about him, aren't you?"

"Junebug, look, now that the police believe Whitney was the culprit, isn't okay to talk to Derek again?"

June asked her what good would come of it considering how Farrah voiced her regret about getting involved with him. Farrah's response had a sane version of heartache compared to Whitney, but it was clear, she pined for him.

"I only want to leave things on better terms. He was nice to us until we implied that he might be a murderer." Not far behind the thoughts of Derek and the hot passion he stirred up, she thought about her husband and what would happen if she could muster the courage to confess.

There wasn't any way for June to talk Farrah out of texting Derek. He didn't reply to her immediately. He let her wait it out or maybe he was busy. She and June loaded their luggage onto the cart Bob delivered to their door. The three of them went to the massage suite to pack everything else up.

"I'll go pull the van around."

Farrah left them at the delivery entrance. Her rubber soles crunched the gravel not moving as quickly as June would have wanted her to. She could smell the cold on the air and hear the distant voices of repressed corporate cubicle hobbits enjoying another rare day outdoors. Her ass vibrated from the phone in her back pocket when his text came through.

Her diaphragm released a massive ball of tension when she read his apology for his behavior. He said that he hated the way they left things and would love the chance to see her before she left. It was the best scenario she could have hoped for. She had been consumed by guilt and worry that another person was angry with her.

She wrote back quickly explaining that she needed to load the van and agreed to meet him in her room before she checked out and turned in the keycards. Informing June of her plan produced predictable results: "do what you want."

She knew June wanted to get on the road as soon as possible. Both of them had been feeling like hostages for a couple of days, but she empathized that June had to be feeling more shook up. She was pissed at herself for wanting another selfish chance to spend time with Derek.

Her thoughts drifted down several possible paths of fantasy. In one, they realized they made a terrible mistake and would remember each other fondly, but never contact each other again. In another, their passionate goodbye lead them to sweaty sex on every piece of furniture in her suite. A third was painful with biting words exchanged where she blamed him for seducing her when he knew full well that she was married. One more dreamy stream of thoughts was pure fantasy where Jackson wasn't even in the picture so they met like average single people in a hotel bar and began an incredible relationship.

Before Farrah climbed into the driver's seat, she unlocked the back doors of the van to make sure it wasn't a mess from bouncing down the road the night they arrived. Everything checked out.

"The board is having an emergency meeting. They need to take action right away because of all the scandals. There's no way heads won't roll. They'll blame anyone possible. Clean house. I don't know what else to do."

Farrah turned around and spotted Sagari pacing between cars. Her phone was mostly hidden by hair, but Farrah caught a look at it. The white case was bedazzled with rhinestones showing off a little personality. She had the impression that Sagari was normally reserved in her behavior but not in her fashion sense which showed hints of flair.

She told herself not to intrude. Sagari ended her call as soon as she realized Farrah was watching her. Chances are the entire cosmetics company staff had taken time to be alone and report back about the unbelievable news of Whitney's arrest and whatever other gossip about layoffs kept them paranoid.

"Do you always make it a habit to eavesdrop on other people's private conversations?"

Farrah closed the van's back doors and apologized profusely. "I'm sorry. Everyone is under a lot of stress. I'm pretty sure I failed in every aspect of my mission to help your employees relax."

"That's never going to happen. Not when we're all about to lose our jobs. Everyone except Brad Dubray, of course."

Farrah offered to give Sagari a ride back to the lodge to save her the half mile trek. She declined and said she'd rather be alone.

CHAPTER THIRTY-EIGHT

JUNE looked bored out of her skull by the time Farrah arrived with the van. Bob helped them load everything into the back, not nearly as gently nor as organized as they had on the trip up.

"If you ladies don't need me anymore, I'll get going." Bob shook their hands, touched the bill of his cap, and departed for other mundane chores.

Farrah dreaded asking June to wait a little while longer, but it had to be done if she wanted to say goodbye to Derek.

The deep sigh June exhaled was a failure in disguising her annoyance. "Yes, sure, whatever. As long as we're stuck here, I'm going to get something to eat. All I had was that pie and I'm pretty sure the adrenaline burned it up."

A whisper of thanks was all that Farrah squeaked out. She reached into her pocket feeling for the thin plastic to make sure the key card was still there and headed to her vacant suite.

It looked different without their things. The maids hadn't been there yet either. She wanted to sit, but as soon as her butt hit the chair, she was too antsy to stay there.

Even though there was staff to do it, she found herself cleaning the kitchenette area. She wiped down the small counter surface and the coffee pot which they had a used a couple of times when forbidden from going to the dining hall. She opened the utensil drawer that the lodge modestly supplied in lieu of disposal plastic. A couple butter knives, steak knives, four forks, four teaspoons, and one large serving spoon. In the next drawer down, she saw the untouched skillet and pancake flipper.

Finally, she was startled by his knock at the door.

"You look amazing." He waited for a proper invitation in before entering.

"I look awful, but thank you anyway. Derek, I'm sorry about the way things seemed and the way the cops treated you." She closed the door and motioned for him to have a seat in the space between the kitchenette and living room.

Instead of sitting, he pulled her close. "You don't have to be sorry for that. They're cops. They were trying to protect you. Wish I could have been the one to do that."

At first, she didn't know what to do with her arms gripped by his strong hands. She hadn't planned it, but her hands found their way to his narrow waist. She could feel the firmness of his core muscles. She remembered them and how the rest of his body felt.

"I didn't need protecting. June did and I still don't know why."

He ran his fingers around her ear a few times. His other hand reached around her back and pulled her even closer. She could smell the scents of vanilla and sandalwood. It was probably something from his soap. She loved every breath of it.

"Tell me about June. What's your relationship like?"

"Right now?" She thought he was going to kiss her again which she couldn't sort out in her swirling consciousness whether she wanted him to or not. Her body wanted him to; her mind didn't. Her mind was mad at itself for the desire. "June's my closest friend. I love her dearly. Why?"

"But she loves you differently? Romantically. I can tell." His hand drifted from her ear to her neck where is fingers glided like figure skaters on her skin. "She's beautiful in her own way too."

"What are you saying?" She leaned back to get a better look into his eyes.

"Nothing. Just an observation. Sorry I brought it up."

"June and I aren't sexual partners if that's what's you're trying to figure out. What is with people projecting onto every single female friendship?"

Farrah was exasperated by every man thinking she and June were sleeping together. Her husband. June's ex-husband. Drunks at the bar. Now Derek. It was inescapable. June reveled in it, but not Farrah. She was exhausted by her neverending effort to desexualize other people's perceptions. It happened every so often because of massage work. She was leery about advertising her services knowing that there'd be a large percentage of people looking for sex workers.

She loved sex. She wanted more of it. But people needed to keep their fantasies in their heads and not displace them onto her.

"You said it. Not me. No need to be defensive." His hand moved down to her shoulder then across her collarbone where a finger toyed with her top button. "Now, where were we?"

She put both hands flat on his chest and tried to push away. All she wanted was a little space between. A reasonable amount. Then she could say goodbye, nice knowing you, let's not do this again.

"No! Derek! That's not why I wanted to see you. I can't!"

Thankfully, he let her go and she didn't need to struggle.

"What's wrong? I thought you wanted the same thing I do."

"No, I don't. I mean, I'm not sure. I have no idea what I want. But I have to sort it out first and that means going home to my family and figuring it out. Please understand."

He released her while she continued to apologize in case she led him on. He persisted. He kept talking about the connection they had.

"You're special to me, Farrah. I can't remember ever feeling this way. There's an invisible bond between us."

"I'm sorry, Derek. But what happened was a mistake. And if you really have feelings for me now, you'll have them after I take some time to figure out my life."

"But we're so connected. We're soulmates. You're in my thoughts constantly." He reached for her hand and pulled her to the loveseat to sit close together. His other hand stroked her knee.

"What about Sagari Palla?"

"Sagari? What about her? She's a coworker."

"Looked like you had a connection with her too." Farrah realized her jealousy was a problem. It got between her and Jackson when he kept having excuses to be out of the house and secret online chats with another woman from the dog park committee. It made her feel like she was trapped in high school again. Stuck in the immaturity of insecurity.

"Are you saying your husband is a problem too? Like June? Someone unwilling to see you for the intelligent, independent woman you are?"

"Uh, um… well… I'm not independent. Stubborn, maybe. But far from independent."

He took her face in his hands and was a little forceful in making her look at him. "Nonsense! You're everything. You're beautiful, smart, a business woman, and a caring soul. You might be a little too loyal to people holding you back though. That's your real weakness."

"Holding me back? Look, Derek…" She pulled his hands off her face. "You might think you know me, but you obviously don't. You don't know anything about my life. June has been my rock. She's saved my ass a thousand times. She and Jackson had to sacrifice a lot when I had legal trouble."

She broke away from his grabby hands and stood. She walked through the room and rested against the kitchen counter. Even facing away from him, she could tell he followed her. She heard his soft steps on the carpet and caught another whiff of his clean, earthy smell.

"I'm not sure June's motives in helping you are always pure. She's selfish. She wants to impress you. To save you. But because it makes her feel good, not for you."

"Isn't that what you said you wanted? To protect me, but the cops were around instead and wouldn't let you."

He closed the space between them. She felt him against her back when he spoke into her ear while stroking the side of her head.

"Of course I wanted to protect you. There's a murderer out there."

She lifted her head but stared straight into the cabinet door. "Was, you mean. There was a murderer out there."

"Right." He nuzzled his nose into the back of her hair and wrapped an arm around her waist. "Farrah, I want you so bad. I need you. I know you want me too."

She couldn't pull away while pinned against the counter. "Derek, no I don't. Not anymore. Let me go! I wanted to say goodbye to you and that's all."

There was a loud beep then clatter. June entered the suite just in time. The disturbance was enough to distract Derek and his grasp lost hold of Farrah. She pirouetted away from him. One hand pulled out the drawer. The other deftly drew out one of the steak knives and pointed it at him.

"Get away from me!"

"A knife? I'm just telling you how I feel. I didn't realize you were so... crazy."

"What's going on?" June didn't back down from Derek's intimidating physique. She bolted directly over to Farrah.

He looked into Farrah's eyes from six feet away. "Come on now. I'm not hurting anyone. We want to be together and we can be if I can get her ass out of the picture!"

June tapped 9-1-1 into her phone faster than she thought possible.

"Hey hey hey! That's not necessary. Put that away. Farrah, tell her. Tell her that you don't need her running your life anymore. You're cutting out the toxic people to be your own woman."

"You're insane! I'm sorry I ever got involved with you!"

It took a minute for June to describe the situation to the dispatcher. Farrah thought for sure, he'd leave as soon as June's call connected, but he stayed and tried to convince her that his delusion was real.

The truth finally hit her. She couldn't believe how dumb she was. It was so obvious. June was right all along. "You were the one who tried to kill June."

"You're damn right he tried to kill me!" June finished giving the information to the person on the other end of the line. She told the dispatcher that they should contact officers Neudorff and Caldwell too.

"June, I'm so sorry I didn't believe you." Farrah kept the

knife pointed at Derek and used her other arm as a barrier to shield June behind her. She was prepared to be June's human shield if it came down to it. Her friend had done so much for her and there was nothing she wouldn't do in return.

He looked at June with seething anger in his eyes. "You. You're ruining everything! She doesn't want you! She wants me!"

"You are a freaking psycho! Let us out of here!" Farrah found herself taking steps back every time he took a step forward.

CHAPTER THIRTY-NINE

THEY didn't have to wait long for the police to storm the suite since Caldwell was meeting with Markos. Seeing his looming figure enter the room gave Farrah comfort she didn't expect. The patrol officers were five minutes away.

It was easy for Caldwell and Markos to tackle Derek to the ground when he opened the door and tried to flee. Back up arrived too.

"Sergeant Caldwell?" Farrah called from a few feet away not ready to leave June's side yet. "There's one other thing I think all of us would like to know."

"And what's that Ms. Wethers?" He saw that the patrol officers had the situation under control. Derek tried to flail a little, but eventually he stopped shouting his nonsense about having done nothing wrong.

She continued to rub June's back in small circles and gave her a final squeeze. She was able to take a step on the plush carpet towards Caldwell.

"You should ask Derek about his wife."

"What about her?"

June interjected as soon as she broke through the tension inside her that had been keeping her relatively quiet. "He killed his wife. He's been telling people she moved to France for a job promotion, but there's no record of her on the corporate websites or basically anywhere at all online."

"Thanks. I'll look into it." Caldwell offered his sincerest apologies for the nightmare they had been through since arriving in what he called, a normally peaceful sanctuary where people came to escape.

June called her attorney when they went outside to watch Derek get taken away. Farrah and Caldwell stood by the rental van positing on the chaos.

"What you're saying is that Milton Byron's murder had nothing to do with your friend's attack? I'm sorry. I thought it was safe to remove the officers from your detail."

"Derek could have wanted Mr. Byron dead too. Several people did. They hold him responsible for the layoffs and ruining people's lives. Derek blamed him for blocking a promotion when he failed to deliver on one of their largest projects. But in the end, both of the attacks were about the same thing - obsession."

"Whitney Gallagher was obsessed with Brad Dubray and this Derek person became obsessed with you." Caldwell pointed in the direction of the patrol cars leaving. A civilian car was coming towards them. It was officer Neudorff on her time off.

"I'm sorry I wasn't the one here to take him down," Neudorff said when she joined them.

June got off the phone and gave Neudorff what passed for a warm greeting. "I wish you'd been here too, but we managed to survive. Can we get the hell out of here now?"

"And never look back?" Farrah added.

"I wanted to make sure you two troublemakers had my info in case you ever do need me again." Neudorff handed them business cards with a handwritten private number. "Or if you want to grab a beer."

*****

Farrah was exhausted when she entered the house. Miles mewed at her from atop the dining room table. The luggage was unceremoniously dropped in a heap. It was the end of a long and traumatic day. She and June managed to return the massage equipment and rental van without another crisis. Farrah sent a message to her boss and explained that she was home but would not be answering her phone until at least Monday.

At six, Jackson came home. He looked at the mess and kept walking. He found Farrah in the living with the TV on and a drink in her hand. Around her, a bunch of used up tissues from the sobbing.

"I have to talk to you." Her eyes were red and puffy. Her voice was muffled by the abundance of mucous clogging her head.

"Me first." He didn't sit. He unbuttoned his coat and draped it over a chair. He bent down to pet Gordon, the lovable beast whose greetings to his master got slower each week.

"What?"

Jackson stood tall and shifted his shoulders back like he needed to muster inner strength. "I went to see a lawyer."

"June has a lawyer to take on the liability cases." She wiped her face. Nothing would improve her visage at that point though and she secretly knew it. Not even all the fancy creams Caressa Lamour had to offer.

Even though Farrah had been planning to confess everything, June said all the gory details would likely come out in the press coverage of the "Retreat of Horrors" as one rag called it. Did he know before she got to tell him? Did it matter?

He crossed his arms over his chest. "Not that lawyer. A divorce lawyer."

ACKNOWLEDGMENTS

There are a lot of people to thank: Joe and my parents who make sure that the cats and I are cared for every day. Neliza Drew, Natali Heuss, Josh Neff who let me be a big ball of stress. The NaNoWriMo Cabin that welcomed me even though they're all horror writers and I don't fit in. Thomas Boatwright, for producing another stunning cover and sharing cat pictures.

I'd also like to thank all the creators who have come on my podcast, Vodka O'Clock, to talk about their processes of making art, writing, acting, and all that entertaining stuff. I find talking to people about their work motivating. I hope that listening to the shows provides that motivation for others.

Lastly, tremendous thanks to the backers at Patreon who have allowed me to be in arts and entertainment.

Cheers,
Amber

ABOUT THE AUTHOR

Elizabeth, "Amber Love" to her friends, is a New Jersey writer and model who openly discusses her life at AmberUnmasked.com and on her podcast Vodka O'Clock. She's written comics, short stories, and a memoir. She's been published in the Anthony Award nominated anthology *Protectors 2: Heroes* and has pieces on the popular websites Femsplain and Women Write About Comics. The third book of the *Farrah Wether Mysteries* is in progress.

If you appreciate a lot of cat pictures and selfies, you're welcome to follow Amber Love on Twitter @elizabethamber and Instagram @amberunmasked.